VERKLEMPT

Verklempt

Peter Sichrovsky

Translated by John Howard

DoppelHouse Press | Los Angeles, California

Verklempt

By Peter Sichrovsky

Translated by John Howard

DoppelHouse Press copyright © 2016

BOOK DESIGN | Curt Carpenter

COVER DESIGN | Carrie Paterson

PRINTED IN CANADA

PUBLISHER'S CATALOGING-IN-PUBLICATION DATA

Names: Sichrovsky, Peter, 1947-, author
Title: Verklempt / Peter Sichrovsky ; translated by John Howard.
Description: Los Angeles, CA: Doppelhouse Press, 2016. Identifiers:
ISBN 978-0-9832540-3-4 (Hardcover) |
978-0-9997544-8-1 (pbk.) | 978-0-9832540-9-6 (ebook) | LCCN
2015943575
Subjects: Short stories, German--Translations into English. | Jews--
Austria--Fiction. | Jews--Germany--Fiction. | Children of Holocaust
survivors--Germany--Fiction. | Children of Holocaust Survivors--
Austria--Fiction. | Jewish fiction. | BISAC FICTION /Short Stories
(single author)
Classification: LCC PT2681.I214 V4713 2016 | DDC 833/.9/14 --dc23

 DoppelHouse Press | Los Angeles, California

FOR COLLEEN

CONTENTS

Pigs Blood

ABOUT AN HOUR south of Vienna, green hills rise out of the flat, deep countryside, becoming steeper and rockier until you get the feeling you have finally reached the boundary between the grasslands spreading into Hungary and the rising Alps of Central Europe.

The villages that were distributed on and between the curvatures of this landscape were popular destinations many years ago, until people discovered the fast lane and searched further and further afield. An hour away from the capital was no longer far enough away for a real vacation.

I spent several summers in this beautiful but boring region and lived in a dilapidated hotel where the owner had made a home for me from three adjacent single rooms and two double rooms. The houses there mostly have large wooden terraces covered and protected from the wind, where on sunny winter days, wrapped up in a blanket, you can dream of times gone by. I often flew to

Germany back then, mostly to give book readings. The flight was paid for, the hotel, the food. So I had my fee, if I had not spent it on an unnecessary sweater or needless pants just to buy something after a book reading to reward myself for mustering enough patience to answer the most annoying questions.

The airport was forty-five minutes away by taxi. In the next village there was a driver with an old Mercedes who always demanded the same fare without ever turning on the meter. He was a small, wiry man, whose age was difficult to estimate, with an eye that never blinked and never moved – a rigid glass ball with skin and an eyebrow that all looked like plastic. The other eye was all the more nimble and cheerful. As though it had to do the work of both eyes, it was constantly in motion.

The taxi driver had one drawback. He talked incessantly. Since I am one of those people who instantly fall asleep during car rides, I tried in vain to keep my eyes open and listen to him, but eventually his words would get lost in my dreams.

Sometimes I asked him a few questions: who lives in that house or how the mayoral election went. I learned the latest gossip from him – who had divorced whom, who had aborted a child, who had been buried.

Once I asked him what had happened to his eye, and immediately regretted it because he replied, "It's a long story."

And he began his narrative with that tragic sentence, which makes you always regret asking people of this generation a question. "You must know," he said, "I was, in fact, in the Hitler Youth!"

But how could I stop him now? He talked and talked, and it developed into a story that was quite different from anything he had told me so far:

I lived during the war with my parents in Carinthia. They were poor farmers, and with the advent of the Nazis, they didn't get any richer. The hope was that everything would change, and I was infected by this hope.

I was seventeen years old and enthusiastic about everything that came our way. But even with the Nazis, there were still the rich and the poor families, and I was given every task in the Hitler Youth the others didn't want to do.

Probably the stupidest job was the night shift. The Hitler Youth had to guard the village and lie in wait for the enemy during the night. They impressed upon us how important this assignment was, and we usually walked anxiously throughout the night in pairs through the dark village, bracing for a hostile attack. We were even supposed to be on the lookout for spies, for stealthy Communists and partisans. In the morning we reported to the mayor, and to lend a purpose to this senseless activity, we made up some suspicious activities, a sound, a shadow. It was just ridiculous.

One night I was supposed to be on patrol with Karl. He was the son of the teacher, a disagreeable little brat with thick glasses and a high-pitched voice. I was to pick him up from school, where his parents had an official residence. He was sick that night, so I had to go alone.

It was not exactly pleasant, to sneak through the village without a buddy to help catch an enemy. Every few steps I turned around. Every sound startled me, and even the trash bins at the roadside seemed to move.

For hours I walked up and down, and nothing happened. But then I discovered a house with an attached garage, and a light was on in the garage. It was about three o'clock in the morning. That was unusual. So late and a light was still on? I quietly crept closer, lay down and tried to look through the crack between the door and the ground. Under the garage door, the ground was damp, a dark liquid flowed slowly outward on the road. I shined the flashlight on the ground and startled. It was blood.

I looked for a place that was dry, where I could see into the garage. I recognized the mayor and his wife. They were slaughtering a pig. A natural matter in a village like ours, but unfortunately, at that time it was forbidden. You could only kill a certain number of animals, and certainly not secretly and at home. Well, I was sure I had finally discovered something really important.

The next day I made my report, of course, to the mayor. He laughed as I told him what I had seen, patted me on the shoulder and praised my enthusiasm. I waited one day, a second day. I waited for his arrest. But nothing happened.

He had committed a crime, it was even a war crime, I thought at the time. A week later the mayor was still the mayor, and no hint of an arrest. Now I was sure he was a spy, who had infiltrated a high position to work for the enemy.

I wrote a secret report to The Reich's Central Office in Berlin. Two weeks later I was arrested and drafted into the Wehrmacht as punishment. I came to Berlin, and after a shortened basic training period, my next stop was Russia ...

He kept glancing at me sideways when he spoke. His right eye, his inflexible, immovable glass eye, could not see me, and so he had to turn his whole face, jerking, fast, and rotate it back quickly.

So now I was in Russia, in a German Wehrmacht's uniform, demoted to the Eastern Front. Recently in the Hitler Youth in Carinthia and now compulsorily in the Ukraine. Back then I couldn't understand how quickly one could become a traitor.

But our great Führer should not have punished me so hard. A young man in Austria, enthusiastic about the war, turned into a hate-filled soldier; only my hatred was no longer directed at the enemy, but instead against my own people. I was going to surrender at the first opportunity.

We were a company made up of Austrians. Once we occupied a village. Great accomplishment! A few old women were still there, who ran off screaming when they saw us. The church on the main square was our headquarters. We sat around, had nothing to do. Some found something to eat, a chicken was fried, a couple of potatoes were dug up. We waited for days and were bored.

One morning, a car drove up, the gate was flung open and an officer rushed in. "Who is in command here?" He roared like a madman, had a red, sweaty face.

I raised my hand. Among all the soldiers I still had the highest rank.

"You will defend this village until reinforcements come, we must hold this position; it's strategically important!" He yelled at me, even though he stood directly in front of me. Then he turned and left the church and disappeared along with his car.

Then I made a snap decision. Only a brief conversation with the others was necessary. Well, unfortunately we had to shoot one soldier who refused, wanted to chase after the officer and report us. All the others agreed that we should surrender as soon as the Russians arrived in the village. We tied a white bed sheet to an old broom that we found in the priests' chamber, jammed the pole in the church door so that you could easily see it, and waited. For two days we didn't leave the church. Then they arrived and took us captive. That was it, goodbye to war and to a heroic death ...

"And your eye? What happened to your eye, if it was all over?" I was curious, not a trace of drowsiness. He made me edgy with his story, the punch line was still missing.

"Wait! My story hasn't even started yet."

"Then I'm going to miss the end, we're almost at the airport."

A good idea and a good business deal for him, I thought, and had to laugh.

"What do you charge for a round trip?"

"Do you want to haggle? With a poor taxi driver from the country, who doesn't know how he can feed his family? No more tourists, no business travelers, and now I'm supposed to go down even more on the special price I gave you?"

"All right, I'll pay, go on with your story. Where did they take you when you were a prisoner?"

"Well, where do you think? The Riviera?"

It was a camp near Irkutsk, we didn't know exactly where. A few wooden huts in a flat area, a barbed wire fence, and all around absolutely nothing. The nearest village ten kilometers away. My interest in cars saved me. I worked in the garage and quickly learned to drive their big trucks.

After a few weeks I had to drive to the village and back every day, and with that my life suddenly changed. I began to smuggle and deal. Transported one thing or another and built myself a small give-and-take network. Along the road were old women carrying large baskets. I stopped, they lifted the cloth that covered the basket a bit. There was bread, potatoes, bacon. They paid me that way for their rides.

I always drove an empty truck to the village and came back with construction supplies. Sometimes I picked up a few soldiers from the train station who had been assigned there. After a month, they didn't even have a soldier come with me. Where could I escape to?

One day I was supposed to pick up a new doctor. I drove to the village and took three women along, which netted me two loaves of bread and a small cut of ham. In the village I waited three hours at the agreed place, until a car stopped next to me and a woman wearing a uniform got out. She lifted her suitcase out of the car, walked up to me and asked if I had come from the camp. By then I'd been speaking Russian for a long time.

She was the doctor. A large, solid woman with dark blond hair and cold black eyes. I tried to take her suitcase. She pushed me away and yelled at me, picked up the suitcase and with a quick, light movement tossed it in the back of the truck, as though it were empty.

During the trip, she didn't say a word. Two women were waiting for me on the outskirts of the village. I didn't know what to do, but then stopped and took them both. They offered bread, I declined.

I was summoned the next morning. When I entered the room of the commander and saw the doctor there, I understood everything. She had reported me.

"And? What about the rest?"

"We're at the airport. Do you want me to pick you up?"

"Yes, of course!"

I flew to a German city with Lufthansa. Next to me, as always, sat dark-clad men, who leafed through important papers with important faces and never said one word.

From the airport I drove into a small town and was met by a long-haired bookseller wearing a beard, who explained to me how difficult it was to run an alternative bookstore in such a small town, but that he considered it necessary to bring writers like me here.

"Why?" I asked him.

Another unnecessary question. He told me about the rise of the Nazis led by the new right, he was surrounded by old and new Nazis here, it was necessary to warn others as soon as possible.

I don't know if it was because he took the curves too fast or because of his words, but I slowly got nauseous.

In the evening, after the book reading, I told the audience that, in my opinion, the new German was a staunch democrat, and should not prohibit right wing or even neo-Nazi parties from having total freedom and that they should have confidence in the new democrats similar to other democracies.

"There will be hope for a democratic future in Germany only when the Germans reject radical parties in the absence of any legal constraints or coercion." I said that every time I wanted to annoy my audience.

I slept in a bad, cheap hotel. The bookseller tried to negotiate a lower fee, and when he brought me back to the train station the next morning, he kept asking me if I was really in favor of legalizing a Nazi party. "How can you say such a thing, you, as a Jew?" He was disappointed in me.

But I was already thinking of something else. During the entire flight back to Vienna, I was looking forward to hearing the story of my taxi driver. He was waiting for me, and as soon as we were in the car, I asked him to continue.

She had betrayed me, the nice doctor with her cold eyes, and I went in the hole. A narrow, low cell, inside of which one couldn't even stand up straight. I had to sleep on the floor and got to eat only once a day. I was furious with this woman and swore to get back at her.

They pushed a pot of inedible muck to me through a slot. I was used to better despite being in a camp. It was all over in a week, and after my release I hoped I could continue my work as a driver. After I was allowed to wash up, however, I was led into the hospital, into the room of the doctor, who was waiting for me. I was furious and asked her directly why she had reported me, what kind of crime had I committed? I told her that I drove the truck every day for months to the village and sometimes took someone with me. I didn't say anything about the bribes.

She sat quietly and didn't say a word. I thought she would realize her mistake, and continued that I had created a special role for myself that everyone had accepted, and that I could also help her if she needed something from the village. Everything seemed fine, she stared at me in silence, and I waited for her permission to leave the room.

But all of a sudden she stood up slowly and walked over

to me. She was just as tall as I was. As she walked toward me, I looked straight into those large, dark eyes, which had struck me right from the beginning. She didn't say a word, and I smiled more out of embarrassment than anything else. She held her hand behind her back. As she stood in front of me, she raised her arm quickly. She had a stick in her hand that I couldn't see before, and she hit me with it. I was completely surprised. We had never been beaten.

She flailed at me and gasped and kept repeating a few words that I didn't understand. I tried to fight back and pushed her away from me. She staggered against the wall, screamed in rage and beat me with the stick like a madwoman. She seemed to have lost all her self-control.

Now I understood what she was screaming. They were names. She said a name every time she struck me. She hit me on the shoulders, on the arms I held in front of the face. I didn't know how to defend myself. Each blow hurt terribly. She was a strong woman, and her anger seemed to give her even more strength. I crouched on the floor, with my hands in front of my face, and could only scream. Then I scooted to the side and had to brace myself. She hit me on the side of my face, right next to the eye. It was suddenly dark all around me. I couldn't recognize anything anymore and lost consciousness.

When I woke up I was lying in a bed with a bandage over my eyes. Everything was dark. I tried to take the bandage off, but a hand stopped me and told me it should not be removed. I recognized her voice and tried to push her away. I was afraid of her.

But strangely, she was calm and friendly, took my

hands away from my eyes almost gently and laid them on the blanket.

"Where are you from?" she asked.

I didn't want to talk to her. She had just tried to kill me.

"Don't be angry," she said to me. "I couldn't help myself, when I saw you and heard your voice. You were the first German soldier I had seen in months. And the first one in internment."

Then she sat down on my bed and told me her story.

She came from a family of doctors. Her father treated prominent party officials and was therefore spared by the KGB. When the Wehrmacht advanced, they had the opportunity to flee. However one of the officials, whom her father cared for, demanded that they stay. The entire family was captured by the Germans. Her father was shot at once, and she, together with her mother and younger sister, were interned in a camp. It was a ghetto. At the time, I didn't know what that was.

Yes, they were Jews. She was the first Jewish woman I had seen in my life. Tall, blond, with fleshy hands, unlike the Jews they showed us in the newspaper in Carinthia.

The rest of the story was horrible, worse than any of our experiences as soldiers.

She assisted the sick in the ghetto as best she could, but it was more a kind of deathwatch. Hidden in a pile of corpses on a wooden cart on its way to a mass grave, she managed to escape. All the other members of the family had died earlier. She made it through to the Red Army, and they had posted her here, far away from the front.

I lay in my bed, blind, blindfolded and asked myself if I would ever see again. And the woman who had beaten me told me her story and asked suddenly for understanding for having treated me in this way.

Why me? Why just me? I asked her. Dozens of officers are here in the camp, and each of them has ordered more crimes than all the ordinary soldiers put together had carried out!

I looked so similar to one of the guards, she said. And the language, it was the language that set her off. This peculiar dialect reminded her of another guard who had been particularly cruel. And all of a sudden she started to yell again, and I was afraid she would beat me. But I couldn't see anything, and could only hear her cries. 'Murderer! Murderer!' she screamed. I raised my arms over my face. But she didn't hit me. I only sensed that she stood up and heard how she ran out of the room.

I don't know how blind people make it in the world. I couldn't do anything without my eyes. An incomprehensible void lay in front of me. This dark hole had no beginning and no end. And add to it a terrible headache. I hated the doctor then. What had I done to her? What did I care about her misfortune?

We arrived at my house in the small village at the foot of the mountain. It was already dark.

"What do I do now? Are you going to fly back tomorrow? Then I could take you to the airport ..."

I interrupted him and said I wanted to hear the story this evening.

We drove to a restaurant. A drunken mailman stood at the bar and welcomed the taxi driver with a hug. But he pushed him away, he had no time tonight, had something urgent to discuss. We sat in the back room and ordered coffee.

"What was her name, the doctor?" I asked him.

"Olga."

"And what else?"

"Only Olga, I didn't know her other names then, everybody called her Olga."

After a week they took off the bandage. It was a strange feeling, similar to the feeling one has when unpacking a gift. You don't know what's hidden in it, maybe you wanted something special, but is that what will unfold?

In that moment, I too had wished for something. And as the layers of the bandages got thinner, I saw light shine through and knew the eyes were still working. And after the last bandage was removed I saw Olga, still quite blurry, but at least I saw her. Well, I don't know, I'm not a poet, but her face was the first thing I saw. And it was beautiful. Unfortunately, only one eye worked. I learned that later. The other, the right, here, this one that she had hit from the side was dead. There was nothing that could be done about it.

Can you imagine how I felt then? At last I've found a corner in this shit captivity where they left me alone. I could drive my truck and do some business on the side. Then along comes this woman, beats my skull in and destroys my eye.

But what can I say? It turned out quite differently. After a few days at least the headache was gone, and I had trained my left eye. The right eye was still bandaged. Olga tried to teach me spatial vision using one eye. That was not so easy. Every day she spent several hours with me, we practiced distance recognition, and one day she even spoke to me in German although, she assured me, she hated this language.

After we got to know each other better, I asked her what she had screamed when she was hitting me.

They were names. All the names of people she had lost and would never see again. I was not angry with her because of the thing with the eye. It had taken a worse toll on her than on me.

After four weeks I was healthy again and could resume my driving duties. Olga asked me if I wanted to continue working at the hospital, she could arrange that. So I stayed with her.

A normal life unfolded in the following weeks. I went to the infirmary early in the morning and returned late at night to my shack. I spent the whole day with her. After a few months, I was driving the seriously ill to the village train station. The old women were back on the road, I swapped bread for a place in the car, and life returned to its old rhythm.

Still, it was quite strange, this situation with Olga. Not the way you think, we weren't lovers. We never touched each other, no gestures, no ambiguous words. We lived and worked more like brother and sister who understand each other and are never separated.

I worked two whole years with her and lived with her in the camp. Although I was a prisoner, I was not alone. The others also accepted that we belonged together. Olga told me a lot about her family, her life in Kiev, and I told her about Carinthia.

She had a lover, one of the commanders. She slept with him once a week. The next morning she came to work, and our lives went on. She sent me out of the room every time she was changing. There was a border, a barrier between us, which I accepted. Besides, what should I do? After all, I was still a prisoner.

One evening Olga took me up to her room. The room was nice, it looked like everyone else's room in the camp, a bare room with a table, a chair and a bed. She pointed to a list that included my name. "You're going to be released," she said, looked at me, and asked if I was pleased.

Released? I had forgotten long ago that I had a home. In the camp I felt like a man who had never lived anywhere else. Olga was there, I had my job and enough to eat. I didn't miss anything.

"So I should go to Carinthia?" I asked her, and I didn't sound very enthusiastic.

"Yes! I've pushed hard for you to be among the first!"

"Will you come with me?" I asked.

She wasn't ready for that one.

She looked at me and smiled. "As for your question, I thank you," she replied. At that moment, she was so beautiful, it was amazing. I wanted to hug her, went up to her, but her face was serious and hard, and she pushed me away.

"Don't ruin it," she said, "your beautiful question!"

The next morning I left the camp. She accompanied me into the village to the train station. We rode in the ambulance. During the ride we didn't speak. The sick soldier who rode with us to the station lay on the gurney and slept. When I got out, she shook my hand and wished me all the best. I wanted to tell her something, something important, but I couldn't. She didn't let me.

A few years later I tried to find her. I worked as a truck

driver and signed up for a haul to Kiev. For three days I looked for her in Kiev, ran from one department to another. It was useless. Nobody knew who she was.

He drove me home that evening. It was getting late, and he didn't want money for the short drive through the night from one village to another. I still left the money on the seat when I got out of the car. ■

The Love Schnorrer

H E PROPPED HIMSELF UP, stared at her face, then the pillow next to her and at the wall above. He knew the painting and the other one next to it. He closed his eyes and his head slumped down beside her like someone had knocked him from behind. For a second, he hated himself.

It was dark, no light shone in the room. The drawn curtains blocked every beam that could come from a street lamp or try to force its way in. His face was still buried in the pillow, turned slightly to the side, eyes closed. He heard the slow breathing of the woman who had instantly fallen asleep on her back. He saw her face without looking at it. He knew everything about her – the stuffy nose that didn't allow air in, the open mouth, the slack jaw, the smell of the matted hair in her armpit. And all over, this muggy, sticky air.

He began to count. One, two, three, four, five.... At eleven he heard her snore. It was always like this, she always snored before the number twenty, sometimes at three or four – eleven was somewhere near average.

He tried to slide off her without waking her, but then knew she wouldn't stir no matter what he did. He moved like some well-oiled part of a machine until he lay next to her, now his eyes wide open so he could see everything in the darkness.

She exhaled with a jerk, threatened to choke, coughed hard and dry, and began to snore again steadily.

He wondered briefly if he would ever dare to strangle her. No, what for? He smiled. Flight is better than fight.

She suddenly rolled on her side, pulled up her knees and mumbled something indecipherable. Even this was familiar.

It would be like it was every time. Now he would get up, go to the bathroom, wash off his orgasm, drink a glass of water and lie down again. Unable to fall asleep, he would turn on the TV, put on the headphones, mute the audio, and surf the channels until he finally slept.

No, not this time! He had something else in mind. He slowly pushed his left leg to the edge of the bed and pulled the right one after it. Leaning on his arms, he moved inch by inch. Leaving the nest of cohabitation became a noise-less game.

He imagined a prison cell. A bunkbed, a sink and a dirty toilet, a bucket of water next to it, no curtain or any other partition in the room. Under the sink, covered by a waterproof sheet, a tunnel being dug for months – narrow, tight, room just for one. It reaches a wide electrical shaft that leads upwards to the roof, to freedom.

The other prisoner – he mustn't notice. There is only room for one – either him or me. He had to be careful.

He crawled out of the room on all fours into the bathroom and dried himself off with a towel without washing. He snuck into his room, where there was a trunk filled with his clothes. He liked this room a lot. Everything was here. A desk, a bed, his books, a radio, a television set and his clothes. He could live in this room, work, sleep. A slot in the door would suffice to push the food through and he wouldn't need to leave for days.

A suitcase lay on top of the trunk. He took it down and carefully put it on the floor, opened it. It was full of underwear, shirts, pants, socks, everything smoothed out and neatly arranged. He closed it and smiled, quietly got dressed, took his passport out of his desk, the credit cards, the driver's license, and all the cash he could find.

And now? A letter? A final word? He took out a sheet of paper, pulled the top off his expensive fountain pen. Was it from her? Maybe last Christmas? Damned Christmas! He threw the fountain pen on the floor. The ink splattered on his pants, on the open suitcase, the white shirt, the underwear – a row of blue dots.

He put on his shoes, slipped on his coat, closed the suitcase and walked slowly to the door. He suddenly stopped, put the suitcase down.

The long hallway from his room to the front door was like a narrowing culvert he had to swim through. A channel with no air, no light, with little chance of ending in the open sea. Doors to the left and right, one after the other, a prison, a hospital, an asylum. In every room lie the half-dead or putrefying bodies. Disgust, fear; get out, just get out.

He stopped, cautiously opened a door and stepped

inside. The room was not completely dark; fish were moving on the walls. They flew around him in a circle, always in the same direction. A lamp with a rotating shade stood on a small table.

Two children slept in two beds – bright, blond children with blue eyes and white eyebrows. Everything in this room was white. The walls blinded, the light was reflected in the furniture; the people looked like they belonged in a Swedish travel brochure. He looked at the two children. Who were they? Were they the wrong ones? From the wrong fold?

He walked slowly backwards and felt for the door handle, left the room and hurried down the long hallway and out of the apartment.

He had parked the car somewhat further away, so no one would hear him start it. Even so, he turned the key slowly and carefully. The engine fired up. It was almost midnight.

After a few hundred yards he began to cry. Cold tears ran down his cheeks. He wiped his nose with the back of his hand and tried to remember the last time he had cried. He couldn't.

There were still seven hours before departure. The on-ramp to the autobahn was just outside the city. The curve was tight, became even tighter, and he was afraid that it would sling him off the ramp. He drove even faster. It pushed him against the door. He could barely hold onto the steering wheel. Now, lift up, fly high and away. But the road became straight, wide, and plunged into a dark hole.

Still seven hours. Three or four of those on the autobahn. He decided not to turn on the radio. He wanted to think one more time about his life, calmly, what was, what would be, what should be. But time itself couldn't be sorted out. Images raced in different directions, no way to hold on to them, spinning here and there and seeming to make fun of him.

What was became the future; what should be no longer existed. Fantasy blurred, no longer as clear as in recent days, hours. All at once thoughts plummeted into this infinite black hole in front of him. And then there was only panic.

He fumbled nervously in his glove compartment until he found a CD, Mozart, a violin concerto. Then it was better, everything evened out; the pointed, angular rocks in his mind became sand dunes, white beaches with soft ground that he sank into as if in flour, up to his ankles. Everything was good; he had done the right thing.

After an hour the highway divided. Two lanes curved right, the other went straight ahead. He thought how little he had to do to move the steering wheel to suggest a new direction. A centimeter more and the tree, the concrete pillars of the bridge – no, it was supposed to be a beginning, not an end.

He was at the airport three hours too early. At a stationery shop he bought three large envelopes. He put some papers in each one, old documents, a bank statement showing a small sum and a passport. He wrote his name on them and the main post office in Sydney. He involved the postal clerks in a long conversation about whether the letters would arrive securely, his name written legibly, stressed how important it was for him to get this mail when he was in Australia. Everything was thought out and planned – nobody would find him there, find out where he really was. In case someone did look for him, it would be in the wrong place.

He had a big breakfast at a cafeteria. Coffee, a soft-boiled egg, orange juice, the rolls were fresh – only a good day could begin this way. He waited at the cash register. The sleepy fat woman with dark dyed hair, white from dandruff where she scratched it, rubbed her eyes, yawned, and kept looking at a clock as though she was waiting for her shift to end. She fidgeted with her trembling, lumpy fingers to put a new roll of paper in the cash register until finally she succeeded.

He smiled, who cares about waiting? Someone who has as much time as he does? A second customer entered this deserted restaurant. He sensed it, heard the tray on the metal slide. It came closer, stopped, moved again until, loud and clear, it was next to him. Only now did he turn to the side and look into her eyes.

He stared at her – wait – what should he hold on to? The tray – it tipped – the orange juice, the rolls, the hot coffee. It soaked into his pants, burned him before every-thing fell to the floor and shards flew in all directions.

You? Why you? he stammered.

I'm sorry, I don't know you.

But we have already ...

May I pay for my orange juice, please? She took her change and went to the back of the empty hall, sat down in a dark corner and drank slowly, sip by sip.

They were still the only customers.

He stepped on the broken pieces. The woman from the cash register came with a dirty cloth, cursed, stooped with difficulty and pushed all the debris under a counter.

He stared at the dark corner. Far away, way back against the wall, he pictured a small head covered with black locks of hair, a narrow face, a white nose spotted with light brown, borderless freckles. Large, light brown eyes, darting, head falling forward.

He couldn't see anything, but she seemed so familiar. She looked exactly like the others in the pictures, the old ones, the yellowed photographs in the albums of his parents. It was actually her!

Do you want everything again? The coffee, the orange juice? Or something else?

He didn't hear the woman and just nodded. She squeezed herself out of the tight chair behind the cash register and brought it all.

As he handed the money to the cashier, he was struck by the wide opening of her blouse. His eyes traveled up and down a long deepening cleavage. The rounded breasts on either side had lost their shape and nothing could hold them in place.

She doesn't look like that, he thought. She has a smooth, tight body, with delicate, round orange halves that look like they are glued in place. He would not lose her. No matter where she was flying, he had to go there too. That was the spark in the darkness, the kindling of light. At last, light. An end to this permanently dull, heavy burden of having lived the wrong life. He knew there was no coincidence.

She abruptly got up, put the tray back and walked past him, looking him briefly in the eye. He had the feeling that when she looked at him her eyes got a little bit bigger.

He took his bag and followed her. When she stopped walking, he would stare into a shop window or seek out a place where he could watch her in a mirror. She was wearing skin-tight dark pants that clung to her slender legs, a black sweater and a black jacket made of leather.

Small and nondescript, she made her way among the people as though she were looking for someone. A totebag hung from her shoulder. It was also black.

Suddenly, she was gone. He had looked into a window for a moment rather than the reflections in the glass. It was a toystore. A train built out of colorful plastic blocks circled along a track, pulling a few cars with yellow, blue and red plastic figures through a tunnel, over a mountain, as a crossing bar was raised and lowered. He had given them the same train set. It was the last birthday. He had sworn to himself that it would be the last one.

When he turned around, she was gone. He hurried through the airport, back to the restaurant, up and down long corridors, even opened doors to the ladies restrooms. He didn't find her. He was desperate. What was the point of this escape, this guilty conscience, the faces of the children?

He continued his search. There were still two hours until his flight. He saw so many small black-haired women, pursued them, passed them, and turned around. They had other faces, but he already thought so when he saw them from behind.

He wanted to pray, beg, plead. He had never done this before. He didn't know any prayers, had no words for him up there who he now wanted to rely on. His escape, wasn't this like a prayer? A tribute to the end of estrangement. Now everything was supposed to be different. He had left the other to look for the one, to become what he should be.

It's over. I'm done, finished. He clenched his teeth. He fought back his tears. Not here among these people. He went to the restroom, locked himself inside, sat on the toilet seat and began to cry. The second time within a few hours. The second time after so many years.

He heard the loudspeaker. His flight being announced. He tried to dry his face with the rough toilet paper. A long line stood in front of his airline counter. He got in line and counted the passengers, seventeen. If each one of them needed a minute, he had seventeen minutes to decide. Either back, not to a home but to everything that had made up the setting of his life for years. Or off to faraway places. But what is the sense in leaving? Now that she was no longer here? Where should he go now? With whom should he start a new life once he gets there?

Only three men stood in line in front of him. He decided to go back. A strange woman was waiting in his house, strange children, but it was a familiar stage, a repetitive drama with no surprises, no interruptions. At least he might grow old and die in peace. The children would become bigger, more robust, and their soft shapes would harden. And the woman? His wife? She would also remain.

He didn't want to think anymore, bent down to grab the bag he had pushed closer and closer to the counter with his foot, picked it up and turned around.

She stood behind him. He almost fell against her. She took a step back and raised her arms, palms facing him but far apart so she would have caught him. This time he spoke to her immediately. When they reached the check-in counter, he took her bag, asked her for her ticket, and requested two nice seats next to each other, if possible in a double row.

And her? She let everything happen, just smiling, always the same smile. And when he asked her a question, she nodded and smiled again.

They sat next to each other on the plane like a couple in love who had known each other for months and now were finally taking their first trip together. It started with a jolt as they raced down the runway, and he felt how his body bore down into the seat. When the wheels lifted up from the runway, he left this barren earth, whose soil was only dry sand for him now.

Two months later they were living in a small apartment on the twelfth floor of a modern building. In a few weeks in the unfamiliar city, he had rebuilt everything, had work, enough money. He sucked the new strangeness through a straw like a parched man and greedily swallowed without tasting what he drank. Everything here was different and yet so familiar.

They had three rooms with a low ceiling, a kitchen and a tiny foyer with some half-rusted iron hooks on the wall. A living room with a dark brown sofa, a low formica table and a painting on the wall.

She had picked out the painting. There were two stripes, a light-blue color and a yellow one under it. Maybe the sky and below it a field, he thought when he contemplated it. Then there was a bedroom with a wide bed and a walk-in closet, and his study.

Everything had been bought in a few days. Not one piece matched another. But the sum of the parts resulted in an entity, a chaotic whole, a system where everything seemed coordinated.

And her? She smiled and was a good woman to him. She kissed him when he went to work in the morning and kissed him again when he came back exhausted in the evening. The rooms were clean, smelled of pine, his shirts were washed and ironed. There was a hot meal every night, and if he wanted to go to the cinema, she smiled and slipped on her shoes and a coat.

She received him every night in her thin arms and pressed his body into herself. Her hands clutched the back of his head and her legs were wide apart. He cried out in pain each time, feeling passion and despair, and afterwards, lying on his back, was certain that his life had just begun.

Two months after arriving in the new town she said one of her few sentences to him.

I'm pregnant.

Are you sure?

She nodded.

She embraced him, and while his eyes stared past her hair to the blue yellow painting, he saw their wedding. A proper wedding. Not the clerk who reads aloud from a worn, black, bound book of laws in a banquet hall with a dirty gray wall and purple curtains that could neither be fully opened nor shut, a room somewhere on the third floor right next to the passport office, the registration office and the immigration police.

And the yellow field under the blue sky in the painting became brownish, earthy, and reminded him of the color of the wall of an old building on a busy street. He suddenly saw this building in front of him again, this building from before – the small information booth just inside the entrance with the narrow door, whose upper part had a sliding window that opened only a crack. You had to tilt your head to be able to speak, and the short, hunchbacked man on the other side also turned his head, and you talked into an unwashed, hairy ear.

Where do you want to go?

To the registrar's office.

His hearing was bad, one had to shout, and all the other people who had entered the building turned around.

To the registrar's office!

Third floor, second door on the left. Next, please.

And this time will everything be different?

A wedding like in the old movies. The chuppah, a broken glass, dancing men who hold each other by the shoulder, a fiddler, maybe a second, a clarinet, an accordion, a singer, two chairs, raised high, with the bride and groom, and between them a small cloth that they both hold by the corners. Everything the way it was a thousand years ago, unchanged and true.

She agreed to everything. It just needed to happen quickly.

Refugees don't have large families, and so only a few friends came to the wedding. Yet when he crushed the glass under his foot, he was sure he had also put an end to his past. She cried, held his arm with her hands and leaned against his shoulder.

They moved into a larger apartment on the ground floor. The building was not exactly new, only three stories, with narrow sliding windows that were hard to open and a rusted fire escape at the back. Yet the ground floor apartment had a small garden and one room more than the old place.

He wasn't sure if he was finally happy and kept asking himself this very question. Now everything seemed right. In his new world, a child was on the way, and it would be different. Brought up differently, it would speak differently, think differently. There was no threat of repetition.

And it grew rapidly inside her. Her stomach soon bulged out in front, as though it were glued on. She ate too little, drank too little, slept too little, and the child sucked everything out of her ever-dwindling body and robbed it of its last reserves.

She looked translucent and boyish from behind, but the child grew ahead of her, and soon her stomach seemed so big it threatened to drop off. She could barely walk anymore and had to support herself wherever she went. Her cheeks were hollow and the skin on her hands slid over her bones when she moved her arms.

He called the doctors, drove her to the hospital, infusions flowed through her veins. Nobody could help her. They tried to calm him down. The child was healthy, and the mother would recover after delivery.

She stayed at home the last few weeks and rarely left her bed. He visited her during the noon breaks and stayed at her side in the evenings. When he opened the door to her room, she lay in half-darkness and he saw the blanket raised by the child, and otherwise all he saw was hair. Only when he got closer did her face appear among the lengthening, dark curls. She didn't want to cut it. It was the only time she said no. They walked a little back and forth in the apartment. He braced her, didn't know the proper way to hold her by her boney elbows.

One day, almost seven weeks before the baby was due, she called him at his office. He needed to come quickly. He reached the apartment at the same time as the ambulance, and they drove to the hospital.

In the ambulance, the doctor examined her and asked angrily why they had not called earlier. Now it was fairly late.

He didn't understand what the doctor meant and tried to defend himself.

They pushed her quickly into the delivery room and made him wait. Later he was allowed to go in and saw her on her back, moaning loudly. A doctor had his hands between her spread, bent legs. A nurse wiped the sweat from her forehead.

He stumbled back into the corner of the room, his hands flat against the cold tiles and listened to his own breathing. His eyes wandered restlessly in this cold room with steel and white towels all around him, and he wanted to get out of there, but the way to the door seemed infinitely long and he would never make the few necessary steps.

He suddenly sensed how his face had become damp and cold. His forehead seemed to separate from his head, and the lower part of his body became heavier and heavier. He slowly slid down the wall to the floor until he sat, slightly leaning to one side, his head against the wall. He saw a large face bending over him, cheeks, lips, amid them a huge nose. Then he saw nothing, felt nothing. In the dark, everything raced around in circles.

He woke up in a bed and saw all the people staring

at him. With an effort, he propped himself up. He had come to without knowing where he was. When he saw the desperate, friendly and compassionate smile of one of the nurses standing around his bed, he remembered everything and knew something had happened.

He jumped out of bed and shouted, Where is she? What happened?

A doctor tried to calm him. Do you feel better now?

Yes, but where is she?

We had to perform a cesarean; the child was too large. She is in the operating room now. Don't worry, purely routine.

He staggered away from the bed, stumbled, afraid to fall again, supported himself until the images in his head calmed down, and wanted to go immediately to the operating room. They took the elevator from the first to the third floor. On the second floor two men pushed a bed into the elevator. He had to move aside. A body was on the bed covered from head to toe. He tried to make out the contours and mounds, where the head was, saw how the sheet lay on the nose and forehead. The mouth seemed to be wide open. The fabric fell naturally into the emptiness. No, it wasn't her. It couldn't be her.

On the third floor, he pushed past the bed on his way out of the elevator. He had to wait in front of the operating room. They wouldn't let him go in. He sat on one of those little plastic chairs, and when he leaned against it, the cheap back gave way. Thoughts from the past tormented him. What had he done wrong? Why this punishment?

Previously, there had never been any problems with the children. The mother was as strong as a midwife; the pregnancies, a natural time of growth, of giving birth, like rhythms of the season.

He remembered the chubby little babies with their greasy, pink arms, nervous, fidgety open hands and huge blue eyes, roaring, with toothless mouths wide open in the thick arms of the mother, wrapped in a cloth, pressed against a huge breast. They were all so healthy, round and fat. Nothing ever had been a problem. All of them ate, drank, slept, sat, stood, walked, laughed, and the world was an amusing puzzle because it was so easy to solve.

He stared at the swinging door leading to the operating room. Behind it, every time another opened, it moved slightly, but nobody came, he had to wait and wait.

Someone nudged his shoulder; he had fallen asleep again. A nurse stood in front of him with a bundle in her arms. He jumped up, tottered, had to steady himself on the arm of the chair. The doctor next to the nurse grabbed him by the arm. They stared at each other for a moment, as if the doctor didn't know how he should apologize.

The pregnancy was more than three weeks overdue. We probably should have induced labor, said the doctor.

She was so weak. Such a beautiful, weak woman, said the nurse. She pushed the cloth on her arm aside and the face of a child appeared. Deep blue eyes, like two glass balls, gleamed in a big, round white face. Then she handed the bundle to him.

He shied back and the bundle almost fell to the floor. He knocked the chair over, the doctor tried to steady him. He took another step back. Why three weeks? I thought it was only seven months! Nine months and three weeks. That can't be right. I've known her for.... He stuttered, he stammered.

The questions thrust into his head like sharp wooden spears. Who was she? Escape? Wedding? Nine months and three weeks? The child? What child? So white and with blue eyes! He retreated again. The doctor and the nurse followed his every step. ■

The Sirens

"HAZEL – HAZEL – WAKE UP – We have to get out – get in the other room –"

"What do you want? Let me sleep."

"Sirens – For God's sake, can't you hear the sirens? I'll get the kids –"

"Fucking sirens. Fucking war. Shit-Saddam – Well, go get the kids."

While Jacob runs to the nursery, the phone rings.

"Jacob – Jacob – Get your gasmask, it's me, your mum! I can see it on CNN – Get your gasmask!"

"Mum? Where are you?"

"Here in Brooklyn – Get your gasmasks! Don't talk to me now – And when everything is over, call me at home, my dear, please come home – But get your gasmask now, I can see everything on CNN –"

Jacob grabs three-year-old Joshua and two-year-old Rachel, carries them under his left and right arms out of the nursery into the sealed living room where Hazel has already turned on the television and the radio. Hazel takes Joshua in her arm and sits down on the mattress that has been lying on the living room floor since the start of the rocket attacks.

Joshua has woken up in the meantime and looks at his mother with big, sleepy eyes. "Do I need to put on that rubber face again?"

Hazel laughs and puts the gas mask over his head, takes the two rubber bands on the side of the mask and briefly pulls at them until they are tight. Jacob gently puts the still sleeping Rachel into a sealed crib.

Then they both take their masks and pull them over their heads.

Hazel feels she can't breathe, and as Jacob nervously gestures to her that something is wrong, she takes the mask off again and sees the small plastic plate that seals the air vent is still in place. She tries to tear it off, but can't.

At that moment they hear an explosion. It sounds far away, but still the whole house moves, and the lamps shake back and forth. A little later, a second blast, a little quieter. Jacob sticks his thumb up, and as far as one can see through the small opening of the mask, he is happy. Hazel, who is still sitting there without a mask, asks: "Does this mean they hit the rocket?"

Jacob nods.

"Well, then I don't need to put this damned thing on."

Jacob nods again, but more agitated and upset.

"I don't want to do this anymore. I've had enough of these theatrics. The Patriots have done their job. The danger is over. I can't stand this mask."

The phone rings again.

"Jacob – It's me again – Are you all right? Is everybody

all right? I saw it on CNN, how the Patriots hit the scuds –"

"Mom – Please! It's not over yet – We still have to wear the masks –"

"Jacob – What? I can't understand you – What happened? Are you hurt?"

"No – But I can't talk with the mask on!"

"Jacob! Hello – Answer me –"

He pushes the mask up a little from his mouth.

"Mother, relax! It's okay – Nobody was hurt – Go to bed –"

"It's five in the afternoon, why should I go to bed now?"

He slams the phone down, jumps up and yells at Hazel despite his mask, that she should follow instructions and put the mask on. The all clear hasn't been broadcast yet.

Her dad's shouts wake Rachel up, she opens her eyes, and when she sees she is under plastic, begins to cry.

Hazel wants to take her out, Jacob turns her way and screams, It is too dangerous, and it might be gas this time!

Hazel pushes him aside, Jacob stumbles and falls on top of Joshua, who howls, rips the mask off his head and hurls it angrily across the room.

In the meantime, Rachel has stood up in the small bed and hits the plastic foil that is wrapped around the bed, screams, throws herself repeatedly with all her strength against the bars of the collapsible crib, until it falls over.

The phone rings. The all clear is given on the radio. Everyone can take their gas masks off, it was not a poison gas attack. The Patriots had intercepted the missiles but the falling parts destroyed many houses and slightly injured some people. The alarm is over.

The phone continues to ring.

Shortly after, the children go back to sleep in their own

beds. The night is quiet, as though there had never been an interruption.

Jacob has calmed his mother down, it is five-thirty in the afternoon in Brooklyn. Mrs. Wertheim sits in the kitchen in a striped dressing gown on an old dark brown wooden chair in front of a small TV on the dining table. A bright bell tone sounds. She takes a cup of black coffee out of the microwave. On the cup, in light blue Hebrew letters is the word Shalom. On the back is a Star of David.

Trembling, she drinks with small sips. The destroyed houses from Ramat Gan are in front of her on the TV screen, ambulances with flashing lights and sirens. "Jacob! Where are you, my Jacob? This should be the Promised Land? For this we have survived?" She shakes her head, tears running down her cheeks, her neck, until they seep slowly into her dry skin.

"Jacob – Turn off the TV!" Hazel tries to pull the covers over her head, but the bright images pursue her, burned into her eyes. Jacob sits upright in bed with the remote in his hand and switches from one channel to the next.

"It can't go on this way. This is the sixth or seventh night, who can stand it!"

"Jacob, please, I want to sleep, I have to get up again in a few hours."

"Sleep, sleep, who can sleep in such circumstances –"

"I could, if you would stop talking –"

"Hazel, let's leave."

"No –"

"Why not, only for a few weeks until it's all over."

"No, I won't run away. We've already talked about this so many times. I'm going to stay here – here!"

"Think of the children –"

"There are other children who have stayed."

The phone rings.

"Hello? Yeah, wait, Hazel is here. No, nothing happened to us, everything's all right – Here, your mother –" Jacob passes her the phone across the bed.

"Ima, what's going on, why are you calling so late? I would have called you if anything had happened –"

"How could you have called me if you were injured? Such a wonderful daughter I have, instead of reassuring her mother, she scolds her!"

"How are things with you?"

"What should be happening here in Haifa, nothing. Besides, we are two old people, your father and I, who needs us anymore?"

"Ima, not now – You know, we all need you, and I'm glad you are doing well. Did you put on the masks?"

"Yes, of course, it isn't exactly difficult."

"And have you sealed up the room yet?"

"No, that's ridiculous. I'm not going to do that anymore. It's bad enough that we both have to sit here with the masks on, but seal up the room, what for? Is this what worries you? You leave us alone here for days, we almost never see our grandchildren, our daughter gets more and more estranged from us with every week that goes by, and all you want to ask about is this stupid seal?"

"Ima, can we talk tomorrow? I want to sleep now, I have to work tomorrow morning at the hospital –"

"Yeah, just sleep, at least you can still sleep."

"Good night –"

"You see, they're worried, too –" says Jacob.

But Hazel was already asleep.

In Haifa, Mrs. Rosen slowly shuffles into her bedroom. She lifts the thin, faded nightgown to avoid stepping on it. Her husband is lying on his back in bed, snoring, his mouth wide open. His long whiskers move easily with every breath he takes. She pulls his blanket up to his neck and tucks it in between the sides of his body and the mattress on both sides. Then she slips into her robe, goes into the kitchen and plugs the cable of the electric water kettle into a socket. While the water gets hotter, keeps simmering and boiling louder and louder, she looks at pictures of her grandchildren, framed, hanging on the wall next to a photograph of her daughter, her only daughter.

The next morning Hazel is paged on the hospital loudspeaker. "Dr. Wertheim, you have a phone call –" She is taking care of an old woman who was admitted during the night with heart problems. A rocket hit very close to her, and the shock wave was so strong that it knocked her to the ground. Now she lies awake after a restful sleep and is doing a lot better. When she wakes up, she takes Hazel's hand, who happens to be standing in front of her bed. "I come from Iraq. I fled from there. He killed my parents, my mother's siblings, only me and my brother he didn't get. He won't catch me now, either. I won't do him that favor –"

Hazel smiles at her and strokes her rough hand, then she hears the loudspeaker. She looks for the next phone.

"Hello?"

"Hazel? It's me, Jacob –"

"What's going on? I don't have any time."

"I've bought the tickets. We'll fly tonight via Zurich to New York to see my mother."

"What? I don't understand –"

"We're leaving –"

"What do you mean, we're leaving –"

"Hazel, be reasonable, we can't wait every night until it hits us. I'll get you in an hour. The kids are at the neighbor's."

"But Jacob...." Hazel holds the receiver in her hand, a bed is pushed past her; she leans against the wall.

She knocks on the door of the director, opens the door and tells him she urgently has to go home, there are problems with the children. She tries to invent a story and, ashamed, feels incapable of telling the truth.

Her boss looks her in the eye, at her reddening cheeks. "Are you coming back tomorrow? You know that our hospital is equipped for a chemical attack. Right now, we can't spare anyone."

Hazel looks at the floor, nods briefly and leaves the room, strides down the hallway leading to her room and pulls off her white coat on the way, hurls it angrily into her locker. As she slips into her jacket, she fights back tears. Then she hastens to leave the building, afraid to run into anyone else, and waits next to the entrance for Jacob.

For a while she sits in silence in the car. "It's for a short time, then we will come back. Believe me, it was a difficult decision for me to make –"

"If we leave now, we are cowards and traitors who betrayed the country and all who have stayed. I know you don't have the same feelings towards this country as I do, but I always hoped you would one day share my feelings.

All in vain...."

"I'm sorry. I admit, I wasn't born here like you and I didn't experience the war as a child, but now it's all about our children –"

"Leave me alone, I don't want to talk. You've been here for five years now, but it has never become a home for you."

"I know, I know, here it comes. I haven't experienced a war, I'm an effeminate New Yorker who lives off checks from his mother, I know all about it – But I don't want my children to be killed by these shit rockets."

"Fine – I accept your decision, but stop talking about it."

They pick up the children at the neighbors and quietly pack several suitcases. The phone rings. "Hi, Ima – Good, I wanted to call you. No, no, everything is fine. Don't ask each time whether a bomb dropped. There would be an alert over at your place, too."

"Well, it could be that the siren didn't work here or we didn't hear it, or some idiot falls asleep on his watch, all kinds of things are possible –"

"Yes, yes, good, good. We're going to New York to Jacob's mother until it's all over."

"What?"

"We're going to New York –"

"What for?"

"Because of the bombs, the rockets –"

"You want to bring my grandchildren to New York where they will be shot by some black man?"

"No, Ima, we're staying in Brooklyn where it's safe."

"You can't do that to me, leave us alone now, and I can't call you there...."

"You can call me anytime."

"I can't afford it –"

"Ima, it's Jacob's idea, I'm going with him. End of discussion."

"For this my parents fled from Romania, for this we made a new life for you, gave you an education, that my child and my grandchildren are shot by the blacks, oh. Almighty, what have I done that this must happen...."

"Ima, I have to hurry, I'll call you –"

"Wait – Hazel, don't go – They'll rape your daughter, and your son will become a drug addict!"

"Ima, Rachel is two and Joshua three. What is wrong with you?"

"Yes, but last week there was a movie on TV, where even children ..."

"Ima, I need to stop now, I'll call you from New York –"

Even the drive to the airport is difficult. Dozens of cars block the road. A black man with a hat and caftan frantically pulls an old shabby suitcase from the luggage compartment of a taxi and sets it down next to three others that don't look any better. His small, fat wife wearing a gray head cloth tries to keep the four children together who are climbing on the suitcases and turning them over.

A nurse pushes an old man in a wheelchair through the automatic doors to the departure hall. The old man pokes the people who stand in his way with his cane.

Hazel and Jacob have finally reached the check-in line.

"This is wrong here, Hazel, we must first go to Security, there's another line over there."

"Whatever you say. I don't care."

"What does that mean? Do you want to miss the plane?"

"Maybe...."

After Security they must get back in line. Jacob is nervous, it is only half an hour until departure. Hundreds or thousands are crowding in the hall, they stumble, curse, yell at their crying children, run their luggage carts against the legs of the people waiting in front of them, old women faint, men pray to their God, and they all want to get away, away from this now precarious Holy Land.

Finally, they sit on the plane. They have taken their seats far back in the last row of the huge jumbo jet. Joshua and Rachel are wide awake from the excitement of travel and run up and down the aisles. A heavily made-up woman between sixty and seventy with a light gray streak in her otherwise dark hair asks Joshua where he came from and where his grandparents were from.

With an angelic voice, he recites the fate of his family: grandmother from Germany, father from America, other grandparents from Romania, the mother from Israel. He has been asked this a hundred times in his first three years.

Next to Joshua stands a slightly larger girl with short brown hair and huge eyes. She tilts her face very close to him and says: "My grandmother is from Morocco, my grandfather from Yemen and my other grandparents from Iraq." She too seems prepared for these questions.

Hazel tries to sleep, but it's useless. Images torment her, sirens, little faces with masks, ruins of the destroyed houses on the TV screen. She sees the black sky through the small windows of the plane. A movie starts. What are the neighbors doing now? Is there another alarm? And I, Hazel, a young Israeli woman, a doctor, three years military service, three wars experienced as a child, am now running away?

After four hours, they end up in Zurich. Jacob drags the sleepy children through the airport and puts them on top of the suitcases on a luggage cart. He pushes them through customs and looks in the hall for the exit to the hotel buses. He reserved a room at an airport hotel when they were still in Tel Aviv. The connecting flight will not depart until the next morning. While they are looking for the exit, Hazel studies the departure board.

Only one aircraft is taking off this evening, destination Tel Aviv. The same plane they flew in on is flying back.

Jacob has found the right bus to the right hotel. He lifts the suitcases into the bus and sits on a bench in the back, the two children on his left and right.

Hazel stands for a moment outside the bus and looks Jacob in the eye, climbs in for a moment and hugs the sleeping children. "I'm sorry, Jacob, I can't go with you –"

"I really hate what you're doing, but please, go back –"

She runs into the airport building.

Five hours later, she lands at the Ben Gurion Airport in Tel Aviv. As the plane rolls up to the arrival hall, a siren sounds. The captain informs the passengers that they will all have to remain on the plane until the alarm is over.

Hazel stares out the window at the dark sky. A white dot moves across the horizon, a second follows it, collides with it, they burst like two light bulbs and fall in a thousand pieces to the ground. Hazel smiles.

She unbuckles her seat belt. ■

Berlin

"A ROOM HAS BEEN RESERVED for us under *U.S. News*." Georg leaned against the reception desk. "Of course. Welcome to the Hotel Kempinski. I hope you had a pleasant flight." The young man in the dark uniform searched the computer for their reservation.

"It was like this," replied Georg. "Seven hours to Frankfurt, a two-hour wait, one hour to Berlin. Quite exhausting –"

"What's going on? I'm dead tired – What about the room?" Cici nudged Georg to the side. Her camera bag was on the floor between her legs. It was never out of her hand.

"So wait for me, sit down somewhere, I'm taking care of the room –"

"Here we have the reservation –" said the man in the dark uniform. "A junior suite with a king-size bed. As requested. Would you please sign here?" He offered Georg a piece of paper.

"What?" Cici asked so loud that some guests turned around in the entrance hall.

"I asked you to sit down somewhere and wait. I'm

handling this!" whispered Georg.

"What is this? One junior suite? And where will you sleep?" Cici's voice was only a touch quieter than before.

Georg took Cici's arm and pulled her away from the front desk. The man in the dark uniform smiled. Scenes of this kind did not seem new to him.

"I wanted to surprise you –" said Georg.

"Thank you, you managed that quite well. No tricks this time. Two rooms or I fly home –"

"Let's try it again. This time, if it doesn't work out, I promise you, never again ..."

"Stop –" Cici interrupted him. She went back to the reception desk.

"Yes?" The man in the dark uniform grinned cheekily.

"Two rooms, one for me and one for him –"

"Of course." He looked again at the computer, gave them two pieces of paper and two keys. The rooms were next to each other on the fifth floor.

They stood in silence in the elevator. Georg stopped for a moment in front of his door and looked at Cici. "You're a cold fish. A blond, pale, cold fish!"

"Thank you!"

Both disappeared into their rooms.

Georg took off his coat and shoes, opened his trunk, hung his jacket in the closet, the pants on a clothes hanger, placed his shirts one above the other in a drawer, the underwear, the socks next to them, arranged his toothbrush, shaving things and hair cream in the bathroom behind the sink, closed the empty suitcase, lay exhausted on the bed and fell asleep immediately.

Cici took off her coat, fell on the bed with her shoes on

and fell asleep immediately.

The phone rang in Georg's room. He jumped up, ripped out of his dream of a family house, children, the wife in the garden hanging up laundry, everything he had always wanted. And Cici should be her. The phone rang again.

"Hi, Who's this? Paul? I don't know a Paul. Yes, of course, you're the writer. I'll be down in ten minutes. Let's meet in the breakfast room. You can have a cup of coffee in the meantime."

Paul looked at his clock. It was 10:15 in the morning. He had been sitting for twenty minutes in the lobby of the hotel. He hated people who were late.

Georg jumped out of bed, ran into the bathroom and turned on the shower. "Damn!" He jumped out of the bath-tub and called Cici. "Hey – Wake up, I overslept – The guy is already waiting downstairs – Hurry up!"

Paul entered the restaurant and sat down at a round table in the far back corner. He ordered coffee and hot milk and a newspaper.

Ten minutes later Georg joined him. "Hello, good morning. I'm sorry. I just overslept."

"Not a problem."

Georg ordered a pot of hot water. He took a tea bag from the inside pocket of his jacket. "I always bring my own tea."

Paul nodded.

Cici turned up a few minutes later and sat down with them. "Good morning!" she said and ordered a fruit tea.

The scene was set. Georg was 48 years old, Paul 45 and Cici 38. Georg was not very tall, he was slim and his dark hair was cut very short, but in back it hung over his shirt collar. Paul had short gray hair, he was somewhat larger than Georg and not quite as slim. Cici was smaller than the other two, had long blonde hair and light brown eyes.

When Cici walked into the breakfast room and headed for the table, Paul stared at her and thought, If she sits down here, there will be trouble.

He was correct.

"I want to get right to the point," Georg said. "We've been commissioned to write a report about the Jewish community in Berlin, with photos. Your books make you an interesting source for us. I'm a journalist, this is Cici. She will accompany us and take photographs."

Paul nodded again. He had become known in the United States because of a book he wrote that dealt with homosexuality in the SS. In Berlin, he worked as a freelance journalist. He didn't like interviews, however, but was too vain to simply turn them down.

Georg took a small tape recorder from his pocket, put it on the table and turned it on.

He asked Paul about the size of the community, where the members came from, how many synagogues there were, how many rabbis, where the kosher restaurant was and if there was a Jewish school.

Paul gave very brief answers to the questions. He looked at Cici most of the time, who was staring bored into nothingness and drank one cup of fruit tea after another. Again and again she returned his gaze, but didn't show any emotion.

"Aren't you going to take any pictures?" asked Georg, who was getting nervous.

"Here in the restaurant? There's nothing here."

Georg continued with his questions. He wanted to know

everything from Paul about the psychological state of the Jewish community. Whether they were afraid here in Germany, how big the problem of anti-Semitism was, how dangerous the neo-Nazi scene was.

Paul became unsettled by these questions. "We, by that I mean my generation, are not victims. Maybe our parents were," he replied rather crossly.

"Yes, yes, but it must have had an effect on the next generation –" replied Georg.

"Of course. But that doesn't make us victims –"

Cici suddenly stood up and said she needed to go back to her room for a second.

"We're going to get married this summer," Georg said as soon as Cici was far enough from the table.

Paul stared at him. They didn't seem like a couple to him. "Congratulations – Does she know about it yet?"

"I haven't asked her, but I've planned this trip so that we'll have a little time together. I've been waiting for this for a long time."

"Well then, the only thing I can do is to congratulate you."

"And you, are you married?"

"Divorced," answered Paul.

"Children?"

"Yes, three."

"I have a daughter. Divorced three times. I was married twice to the same woman," said Georg.

"Sounds familiar," Paul muttered so indistinctly that Georg could hardly understand him.

Then they both fell silent. Not another word about Jewish culture, the Jewish community or neo-Nazis. Georg fiddled with his tape recorder, turned it on and off, listened to the conversation he just recorded.

Cici came back. "Are you finished with the interview?" she asked.

"No, but now I've got to leave for a minute," Georg said as he got up.

Paul waited a few seconds. "Congratulations," he said.

"Okay. What for?"

"Your engagement –"

"What?" Cici was dumbfounded.

Paul explained to her what Georg had entrusted to him.

"He's crazy, that clown – That's complete nonsense. I need to have a talk with him. This can't go on! For months, he's been trying to convince me that we're a perfect couple – I'll be right back."

Cici got up, left the breakfast room and left Paul alone at the table. He listened to them arguing in front of the door but couldn't understand what they were saying. After a few minutes they returned to the table and sat down. Georg turned on the tape recorder again.

"How does it feel to be the son of a survivor in Germany?" he asked.

"He already said he doesn't feel like a victim," Cici interrupted.

"Why are you butting in, you don't know anything about anything. No surprise, how could you understand the feelings of a Jew? You don't have this in your family history –"

"What do you mean by family history? Yours? What did your father do during the war? He wasn't even a soldier, sat in his mansion in sunny California and played catch with you in the garden every Sunday afternoon until you were both so sweaty and tired you had to jump in the pool! What do you know about concentration camps?"

"Like I said, you don't understand – You come from the wrong background!" Georg was enraged and his voice kept getting louder.

Paul had leaned back and was listening to them.

"Am I right," asked Georg, "that there's a shared commonality among the Jews where the Holocaust is concerned?"

Paul shrugged. "I don't know," he told Georg. "My father went to England and was in the British army. He came back to Germany as a conqueror. I always tell the joke that my father won the war. Survivor? I'm not the son of a survivor. He lost his family in the camp. That destroyed him. It probably had an influence on my life. But about being children of survivors? I don't know."

"This is a joke –" Cici was getting agitated. "There's one whose father was in the British army. The other one whose family never left California during the entire war. But both of you are victims – And what about me? My dad was in the U.S. Army! The Germans took him prisoner and he almost croaked in the camp where he had to eat rats for two years and lost half of his buddies. After the war he was so messed up that for decades he tyrannized us kids and my mom. The only child of a survivor present and accounted for is me!" She was yelling so loudly that everyone in the restaurant turned around. There weren't any guests remaining in the breakfast room. A couple of young women wearing light brown uniforms bussed tables. One of them came to the table where the three of them sat. "I'm sorry, but breakfast is no longer being served."

"What do you want? Why are you butting in? Are we maybe too loud for the Germans around here?" Georg jumped up and yelled at the young woman, who was so frightened she took a step back.

Paul laughed out loud.

"Why are you yelling at this poor woman? She's maybe twenty-five," said Cici.

"The Germans are all guilty," Georg blurted out.

"Yes, all of them – They are also responsible for the corns on my feet, because my father was too cheap to buy me new shoes so I had to run around in shoes that were too small. And why did he do that? Because the Germans tortured him in the camp." Cici's voice cracked.

"I have to leave again. All that tea, I'm not used to it," said Georg, got up and left the room.

"That's ridiculous, what Georg told you," whispered Cici. "We aren't in a relationship. We have never been a couple. Georg kept wanting to, but I didn't. That business with the wedding is complete nonsense –"

"It's okay, doesn't bother me in the least; you can do whatever you want –"

"Why? Is it all the same to you?" Cici looked him in the eye.

Paul returned her look without saying a word.

"And?" she asked.

"If I were ten years younger, I would run away with you," said Paul.

She smiled. "And today? Do you feel like you're too old?"

He nodded.

"And love? What about love?" Cici asked him.

"I lost that somewhere along the way. Today I just want a butler who shines my shoes and cooks a soft boiled egg for me in the morning."

"Idiot," hissed Cici quietly.

"Why? Are you going to prove me wrong?"

"I don't want to prove anything to you – At best, I would like to kiss you." She saw Georg returning and pushed her foot against Paul's leg under the table.

"I need more information," said Georg as he sat down. "The identity of the Jews here, that's the most important theme for my work. The children of the victims live together with the children of the victimizers in a city and..."

"And are even married sometimes! And have children who aren't just half-Jews, but also half-victimizers and half-victims," Paul interrupted.

Cici giggled.

"You see – You don't understand this! You wouldn't laugh about it if you did," said Georg.

"So what? Did you mean that seriously? All that victim-victimizer nonsense?"

"Of course we are victims," said Paul. "But victims of our parents. They came back to Germany, not us. Now we have to live with their guilty feelings and those of the Germans. Who can live a normal life here?"

"What a sorry bunch – Three children of survivors. And each one has a reason to feel sorry for himself," said Cici.

"Maybe that's why we get along so well," said Georg and glared at Cici.

"I believe I have to excuse myself now," said Paul and got up.

Georg watched him go and waited. "How can you do that to me? In front of him?" he asked.

"Do that to you – You tell him this bullshit about us getting married!" Cici got louder again.

"Don't yell like that! I know what you want – We would get along so well –"

"Georg, why can't we just be friends?"

"I can't do that. It's either all or nothing. Tell me that you don't love me, and I'll never ask you again."

"Good, my dear, if you insist: Georg, I don't love you!"

"You don't mean that."

"Yes, I do!"

They jumped up, circled the table and yelled at each other. The young women in the light brown uniforms began to prepare the tables for lunch. Paul returned. He had overheard them from outside. All three sat back down.

"What's wrong with you two?" asked Paul.

"This has nothing to do with our work here. Let's go on with the interview," answered Georg.

Cici got the camera out of her bag and started taking pictures of Paul. She stepped back a few steps, got up on a chair and shot a few photos.

"Have you thought about emigrating?" asked Georg.

"Sure, all the time. The question is not so much where to go as with whom to emigrate." Then he turned to Cici, looked directly in the camera and said, "Or *to* whom."

Cici lowered her camera and smiled at him.

"You can't possibly live here – With the people who murdered your ancestors," said Georg.

"What nonsense! I live with the post war generation. They didn't do anything –"

"But they are somehow guilty, too."

Cici got down from the chair. "There you go again with the crazy talk – What did they do? Are you responsible for what happened in Vietnam, Georg?" asked Cici.

"You can't compare that with the Holocaust –"

"Good, maybe you're right. Then the young women here in this restaurant are also responsible for my miserable childhood – My father was an emotional wreck after the war. Because of the Germans! So they're all guilty – Can you see how crazy that is?"

"I'm sorry, I don't want to intrude," said Paul, "but there is something absurd about your fight. Maybe this is about something else?" Georg and Cici looked at him. Nobody said a word. Cici broke the silence, got up again and resumed shooting photos. She slowly walked around the two men and pointed her camera at one of them and then the other. While Georg stared into the cup of coffee he was holding with both hands, Paul turned his head as he tried to follow Cici's movements.

"How's your love life, if I may change the subject?" Cici directed her question at Paul, while she kept shooting one picture after another.

"Shitty," Paul answered.

She laughed out loud. Paul laughed, too.

"Here we are, sitting together in Berlin. Each of us trying to make a war that was over a long time ago responsible for everything, but basically we're only lonely and pining for love," said Cici and she pointed her camera directly in Paul's face.

"That's enough for me!" Georg got up. "I can't work like this. We have an assignment, in case you've forgotten," he said to Cici, who stepped back, startled.

The young women in the light brown uniforms had set all the tables for lunch. But they didn't even approach the table where Paul, Georg and Cici sat. A waiter dressed in black came to their table. "Would you perhaps care to order something?" he asked.

"What?" Paul looked at his watch. "Is it noon already?"

Georg muttered something about wasted time and turned off the tape recorder that was on the table and had been on the whole time.

"Why not?" said Cici and sat down. "Why don't we just eat here?"

The waiter brought them menus. Paul ordered a broiled chicken, Cici and Georg a vegetable plate. They spoke awhile about the food in the United States and in Germany, but quickly tired of the subject.

"I don't want a stable relationship anymore. All I need are a butler and a girlfriend who are exchangeable," said Paul.

"Rubbish – You can't have a good life without love," Cici countered.

"Can we talk about the Jewish community here in Berlin?" Georg interrupted.

"Okay," said Paul.

"Was your wife a Jew?" asked Georg.

"What does that have to do with the community?" asked Paul.

"I only want to address the problem of mixed marriages. Everyone is talking about this in America."

"I'm not going to talk about my ex-wife here."

"Why don't you tell him about your ex-wife times two? Twice, the same non-Jewish wife – That's quite something to add to the conversation," said Cici.

"I can't work like this! Can't you understand? We have flown for hours to get here, it was expensive and time consuming. Now we have to think about our assignment!" Georg was furious.

"I wasn't the one who started talking about relationships," replied Cici.

The waiter brought the food. They talked again about different customs of eating, the quality of the hamburger, the steaks, the different types of bread in the United States and in Europe. After lunch, Georg got up and left the room.

Paul grabbed Cici's hand. "I don't say this very often, but you are so very beautiful. Let's go up to your room."

"Are you crazy?" She laughed.

"Then come, we'll run away!"

"Where to?" asked Cici.

"Who cares?" He slowly stroked Cici's forearm. She didn't pull away. His face came closer to hers.

"No, don't – If Georg comes back now –"

"Who cares?"

"I can't do that to him."

"The poor thing – A victim after all?" Paul grinned.

"Are we both damaged by the war? Our fathers fought in the war and handed the trauma on to their children? My family was pretty wrecked," said Cici.

"And Georg is the only one who comes from a normal family? Is that why he married the same woman twice?"

Cici saw Georg approaching. She scooted away from the table.

"Can I speak with you alone for a moment?" Georg asked Cici.

"Okay, then I'll go outside –" Paul got up and left.

"I can't stand the way you are flirting with this guy," Georg said.

"That's ridiculous –"

"You can't do that to me."

"Funny, I just said that to Paul. Let's say, I like him. Why not? Am I in a relationship?"

"I couldn't accept that – Not him! Not here –"

"What are you saying?"

"I'm warning you, I couldn't stand it – It may be that you would lose your job –" Georg stuttered a little from sheer excitement.

"You can't possibly mean that?"

"Oh yes! Not with him. With anybody else!"

"Why?" Cici's voice got louder.

"Not a..." Georg choked.

"Well?"

"Not another Jew! And especially not this ridiculous writer here with his stupid book. What can he offer you that I don't have?"

"Probably nothing, you're right about that, absolutely nothing, except maybe a life."

"You're dreaming! He could never support you. He is probably as poor as a church mouse, lives in this dirty town. What is this all about anyway?" Now Georg was getting louder.

"I'm asking you for the last time, let me be – If you don't, there's going to be another catastrophe here!"

Paul came back. Another moment passed without anyone saying anything. The waiter asked if anyone wanted coffee. They ordered coffee, hot water and a fruit tea.

"Well, what are we going to do now?" asked Paul.

Neither one of them gave him an answer.

"No more questions about Jews, Nazis, the persecuted,

victims or victimizers? Perhaps we should talk about relationships? This is an interesting triangle story," he added.

"I don't think that's very funny. I have the feeling you are
both making fun of me," said Georg.

"That's so pathetic," said Cici.

"I don't want to meddle in your relationship..." Paul tried
to calm Georg, but Georg sullenly waved him away.

"I'd like to be alone with Paul for a minute," Cici suddenly
said.

"Why?" Georg asked.

"I just want to – I don't have to give you a reason –"

"What do you want from him?"

"Please, don't make a scene, just ten minutes. Go to your
room, I'll call you and then we can leave this hotel before
we have dinner here, too."

Georg got up without a word and left.

"And? What now?" Paul asked.

"I don't know."

"Why did you send him away?"

"I wanted to be alone with you –" Cici scooted closer to
him.

"I'm glad he's gone –"

"Me too," said Cici and looked Paul in the eye.

"Should we just run away?" Paul asked.

Cici nodded.

"Without telling anyone? Like I might have done ten
years ago?"

Cici nodded and smiled.

"But I only want a butler."

"What do you do in the evenings when you're alone?"
asked Cici.

"I yell at him when I'm in a bad mood –"

Cici ran her fingers through his hair. "Such a bad little boy."

"Come on, let's get out of here," said Paul.

They left the hotel and walked down the Kurfürstendamm. They wandered through the city for hours until they were suddenly standing in front of Paul's house. There she spent the night. When they returned to the hotel the next morning, Georg had already left. He didn't leave a message. ■

Clearance Sale

"MOM, MOM, guess what – I've done it!"
"What, what have you done?" She sounded tired. It was nine o'clock, and she had slept badly.

"They promoted me."

"Fired – what? Again?" She sat up and pushed a cushion behind her back.

"Promoted!" He screamed into the phone.

"Primo, don't shout!"

She called him Primo. He was her first and only son.

"The director called me to his office this morning. I thought, God knows what's gone wrong again. But then, imagine this, I'm the new head of the Children's Department."

"The what?" She rubbed her left shin bone with her right foot and pushed the thick covers aside. It was always either too cold or too hot. The bedroom window was closed because of the pigeons in the back courtyard.

"The Children's Department – Yes – I will manage the

entire department all by myself with six employees. Well, what do you say now?"

"And you woke me up for this?"

"Screw this –" Primo hit the table with the receiver. He had waited half an hour in his office on the third floor of the Zweibach Department Store before he called her so he wouldn't wake her up. Ever since she got her cable TV, she had been watching old movies until the wee hours, and slept half the morning away.

"What did you say? I can't understand you."

"Nothing, mom. It's okay. I'll call you later."

He hung up. Why did I call her, he thought, why bother? Why didn't I call my wife first? He dialed a new number.

"Hi. It's me –"

"What do you want?"

"I've been promoted! I'm head of the Children's Department –"

"That's great – I'm so happy for you. Can you pick up the kids today? I've got a seminar this afternoon, and it's going to run late."

"Listen, Gertrude – I'm head of the Children's Department now. I'm in charge of everything – all by myself –"

"Yes, I'm really happy for you, but I can't pick up the kids – You need to...."

He hung up. He recalled an image. In the mountains somewhere in Tyrol. It was summer. The road wound in tighter and tighter as it curved up to the peak of the mountain. He looked at Gertrude, who was holding the steering wheel like a truck driver. Her dark blonde hair pulled back tight, her eyes as bright as water, and her white skin without blemishes. She drove the car calmly around the curves almost without shifting.

Reassured, he leaned back and fell asleep. When he woke up, they had reached the mountaintop. Gertrude stood next to the car and stretched. He got out and stared at her small, firm nipples that strained against her dress.

"Will you marry me?" he asked.

She laughed, took his hand and ran across the meadow until he could no longer follow her and fell to the ground exhausted. She ran further and further to the end of the meadow. For a few minutes he didn't see her, then she came back and dropped down beside him. She lay sprawled on her back and tore clumps of grass out of the ground.

Instantly, he was all over her, on his knees between her legs, and tried to open his pants. He heard her gasp as he rolled back and forth on her like a round potato.

"Wait, that's not going to work," Gertrude said, and took the matter into her own hands, the way she always took everything into her own hands later.

In the week following this trip he introduced her to his mother on a Sunday afternoon when, as always, his sister, her boyfriend and two aunts dropped by for their weekly visit.

"Primo, she's a beautiful woman. That's true. But why do you need to marry her so fast?" she whispered loud enough for everyone in the room to hear her.

"It'll be alright, Mom, believe me –"

"No – You believe me! It won't work out – Her father is for sure big and blonde, all her mother ever wears is a Dirndl, and in the bookcase in the living room there is still a special edition of *Mein Kampf* they got for their wedding –"

"Mom, it's 1985 – All that is over –"

There was another knock at the door. Primo closed his eyes. He jumped up and shouted, "Yes. What is it?"

There was another knock. Primo shouted, "Come in!" Another knock. He went to the door and opened it.

He looked at the opening of a dress, as large as a dam between two Alpine rivers that had formed two large lakes. Her skin was white, and he saw peach fuzz on her two breasts. Two large brown eyes stared at him.

"Am I in the right place?"

He smiled. "It depends –"

"I want to see the head of the Children's Department."

"Then you're in the right place. I'm in charge here, and have been for exactly one hour."

"I'm supposed to report to you."

She took a step towards him. He stepped back. Her colorful dress stretched over her body, and her breasts swayed with every movement like a pendulum swinging from left to right.

Primo was fascinated. The girl came right out of a story he had read way back, and now she had strayed here. He took refuge behind his desk. She followed him and sat on the edge of the desk and looked down at him.

"My name is Maria Seifert, and I'm your new assistant. I applied for the position right away when I heard that you are taking over the management of the Children's Department."

He nodded.

"I used to be in the Ladies Department. But I was told I wasn't a good fit there." She smiled and ran her hands over her body from her breasts down over her stomach and her thighs.

In that moment Primo knew things would not turn out

well. But he didn't want to put up any resistance. "Your name's Maria Seifert?"

She nodded. "But that's just my married name. My family name is Rosen, I was Maria Rosen. I don't know why they gave me the name Maria, doesn't really suit me at all."

"Why? I think it's very beautiful," Primo protested. He thought it was ridiculous, but what should he say in front of this statuesque woman? "Come on, I'll show you everything –" He wanted to get out of his office.

She slowly slid off his desk and steadied herself with her hand on his shoulder.

"Whoops – I almost fell –"

He felt the weight of her body through her hand, didn't move, waited until she had walked around the table. He stood up, made a detour around her, and opened the door.

They strolled through the department. Primo showed her the stuffed animals, the dolls, the racing cars, the Lego sets. He explained the storage system, the inventory, the re-ordering procedures. The sales girls greeted him warmly and congratulated him on his promotion.

Maria introduced herself to them all. "I'm the new chief-assistant, Maria Seifert!"

During his lunch break, he drove his car to the kindergarten, picked up his two daughters, Lisa and Barbara, drove them home where a student was waiting to babysit them until he came home. The children cried when he left. They hardly knew the student and didn't want to be left behind with her. Primo promised to bring them a surprise if they would stop crying. Lisa, the eldest, held on to his jacket with both hands and begged him to take her with him to the office. "Can't do it this time," he said and felt miserable.

After his lunch break, Primo found his office completely rearranged. His desk stood opposite the door at an angle so he could see the window that was previously at his back. A small carpet was in front of his desk on the dark wooden floor, and two chairs were missing. In another corner of the office, he noticed a small set of leather furniture: a couch, an armchair and a low, round table. Yellow flowers stuck out of a thin blue vase in the middle of the coffee table, and on his desk in the right front corner was another vase with flowers. Primo sat down in his swivel chair and leaned back. The chair was also new, moved in all directions, and the leather upholstery smelled like brand new shoes.

"Like it?" Maria asked.

"Who told you to do this?"

"Nobody, I just thought..."

Before she began to cry, he reassured her and told her he was very happy about the changes. In the future, though, she should ask first.

She nodded and left his office.

It was Friday, and he wanted to leave his office early. The children were taken care of. Gertrude would come home late from her seminar, and he had promised his mother he would spend this evening with her.

It was his father's *Yahrzeit*. He intended to go to the synagogue with his mother and afterwards to the kosher restaurant next door. As he did every year at the synagogue, he would lean with both hands against the metal plate on the wall and recite a prayer in the memory of his father. That was all he could do for him now.

The phone rang.

"Yes, oh, it's you."

"Listen, my seminar is taking a little longer again today. Can you pick up the kids or not?"

"They are already home –"

"Okay, can you relieve the baby sitter? I'm coming home late for sure."

"No, I have to..." He hated these discussions and always felt he was playing the role of a poorly represented defendant. "Today I have to..."

Should he tell her the truth? If he told her what he was going to do she would yell, berate him, and, insulted, hang up because he hadn't invited her. This is typical, she would scream at him, this constant going off on your own, setting yourself apart, no wonder this family never unites and so on and so forth. But which excuse would work now?

"I can't. It's my first day as head of the department. I have to stay until closing time."

"That's ridiculous – You're the boss now! But you're lying to me. This is the *Yahrzeit* for your father. I phoned your mother. I don't need you to pick up the kids. I just wanted to see what kind of excuse you would make."

"No, no. I'm sorry, you can come, too, but you always feel so funny there, so strange."

"I don't feel strange. You feel strange with me there in your little world."

"No, that's not true –"

"You know what? Kiss my ass –" She hung up.

Primo got up and left his office. It had been this way for five years now. Five years, two children, a mother-in-law who wears a Dirndl and still has her photo of when she was in the *Hitler Jugend*, a father-in-law, big and blonde. Just as Mom had predicted. The only thing that had changed was that he sat behind the wheel now when they drove and she slept. He looked at the clock. It was three o'clock in the afternoon; he needed to go home to change clothes. It was winter, the sun went down early, the day ended long before the evening began, and the service would start soon.

The third *Yahrzeit* for his father, who had abandoned him when he was so young without leaving anything behind. He had never had a father, maybe a nice uncle who went for a walk with him once a week. Primo was not five years old when his father fell in love with a young employee at his business. She was called Brigitte and was as Jewish as the Pope. She was reformed for a few thousand dollars, accepted by a liberal community in New York, and from then on she was kosher enough to be Primo's step-mother. Many years later she robbed the pubescent boy of his sleep during the nights he spent at his father's.

Primo walked past the shelves crammed with toys and thought about Maria and not about his father.

"Excuse me –"

Someone tapped him on the shoulder. He turned around and found himself starring once again into a décolleté that revealed much too much.

"You can't walk around here like that. There are children and parents here –" he said.

"What do you mean?" Maria stood in front of him and smiled.

"You know, this décolleté. You can see almost everything –"

"I'll put on something else tomorrow. I promise. I only wanted to remind you that you have to leave earlier today.

The *Yahrzeit*, you know?"

Primo froze. "How did you know that?"

"It was on your calendar."

"And? Do you have any idea what that is, *Yahrzeit*?"

Embarrassed, she looked down at the floor. It didn't work. Being embarrassed didn't suit her. "I've already told you my maiden name is actually Rosen. I understand you. I know about this ... even if my husband doesn't ..."

"I didn't know that you ..." he interrupted.

"Yes, you can say that. The papers have been lost. The papers of my mother, but I have always felt that way."

They looked at each other for a few seconds, and their eyes bore deeply into one another's. Then they wandered through the corridors of the department, past the Lego bricks, the Barbie dolls, the teddy bears and the water pistols, and told each other their stories. Being married to the wrong person, he as well as she, the alienation, the longing, the misunderstanding, the children and the never-ending loneliness. Compassion and understanding connected them like a brother and sister who had found each other after being apart many years.

Later they had a cup of tea in the cafeteria, ate cakes, laughed, and as if by chance touched each other's arms and hands. Hours went by and Primo ignored the announcement that kept calling him to answer his phone.

It was after six o'clock when they came back to his office, and he knew that it was too late for everything: to relieve the babysitter, to go to the synagogue, to pray for his father, to take his mother to dinner. He missed everything. He felt guilty, and he felt good about that.

"Maybe we should spend the evening together? We can

go to the restaurant where my mother is waiting."

Primo imagined the scene. The table set, the silver cups filled with wine. His mother, Maria, and he. Everything suddenly fit together, a perfect picture, and everyone would understand without having to explain anything.

"Maybe next year," he said quietly and smiled.

"Yes, maybe," Maria whispered.

He locked up his office. The department store was already closed, the last customers and sales staff had left the building. They were alone. They went slowly through the great hall that had the stuffed animals. Maria sought his hand. He didn't pull it back, reached out for her, tried to hold her, but her body was too big.

She nudged him to the side with her elbow. When the lights suddenly went out, he let his briefcase fall. It must have been seven o'clock. The service at the synagogue was ending.

Maria pressed him against a gigantic teddy bear that slowly sagged and fell on its back. Primo let himself be thrust onto the bear's stomach. Against his back, he felt its soft fur. Maria was on him and slowly unbuttoned her dress, until a white mass flowed out and spread over Primo. He lay quietly and did nothing, no kiss, no movement, no touching. His hands hung to his left and right.

Maria gasped and moaned, grinding back and forth. She put her nipple in his mouth. He searched with his hands, didn't find anything but her dress. She took his right hand and showed him the way, guided his movements.

She suddenly pushed him away and stood up. Like a monument, thought Primo as she stood in front of him, tall, wide, long black hair and a half-open dress.

"Come on, take your clothes off –" she said. Her voice was very different than before in the office. It sounded like a sharp command.

"Here?"

"Yes, here –"

Then she got on her knees and tried to open his pants. He wanted to do it himself, but she shoved him away, undid his belt, the button, and pulled down the zipper. With one jerk, pants and underpants were at his knees, and she pulled everything down together with the socks and tossed the clothes away in a high arc.

She laughed out loud, turned him on his side, and ripped off his jacket.

Primo remembered a diaper scene with his children. Somewhere in a restaurant, an airport. The child cries, its nappy wet, he puts the baby on its back on a towel or just the carpet, opens its pants, the shirt, turns the child on its side, lifts it up, pulls down the wet nappy, lifts the child with his hand by both legs and pushes the dry nappy under the small behind with the other hand.

Now he was lying on his bare back on the stomach of a teddy bear, his undershirt his only protection. Maria knelt before him and tried to awaken what was still asleep on his body, but it didn't work. "Don't worry –" she told him, "We'll get it up –"

He didn't worry. He lay quietly and stretched out on the soft fur and felt cold. His thoughts were with his father, who had taken the other path from the familiar to the unfamiliar; left his mother with their children and ran off with this young, blonde, thin salesgirl who made him happy.

Home, what was that? A woman? A house? A city?

Mother? Father? What else would he have to leave behind to arrive at last?

Maria kissed him all over – his toes, the soles of his feet, his heels – slowly slid her tongue along his leg, pushed up his undershirt and sucked on his nipples, his ears, kissed his neck, his arms, pressed her breasts against him and kept whispering how horny this made her feel. His body was a home for her. She felt she had arrived and was, at last, understood and accepted. How many years did she have to spend in bed with a man who, disruptive and strange, got lost in her body? Now everything was different. She would prove to him that she alone would make him happy.

And Primo believed everything she said. He was grateful she was on a campaign to recall his faulty product, stretched his legs and tried to find a position on the bear where he simply felt good. But all the caresses were in vain. Primo was unable to get aroused and Maria was becoming impatient.

"Wait, we'll try something else –" she said. She got up, gathered up her dress, turned around and climbed with one leg over the bear. Primo looked up but couldn't see anything in the dark. Everything was black and covered with thick hair; Maria didn't seem to shave even her legs. She slowly lowered herself until she touched the floor with her knees, plunged at what Primo had between his thighs. At the same time, she slowly lowered her ass and rubbed it on Primo's face. Her movements became more and more hectic and tense, and Primo visibly responded to her treatment. Maria could feel how her juices were getting more and more concentrated, and she pushed her pussy harder against Primo, whose head was thrashing back and forth and almost drove Maria into a frenzy.

But he was desperate because he couldn't breathe. He wanted to push her away, dug his fingers into her thighs and tried to turn his head to the side. He felt her sucking lips, the tingling in his loins, and forgot about breathing and about the mountain that he wanted to move. For a moment he thought it was maybe his destiny to die this way, but then he tried one last time using all his strength to push this woman off of him.

Everything happened simultaneously, the way both of them had always wished and never experienced before. Primo was the first who could not hold back or control anything anymore. He pushed himself up from the floor, desperately shoved his loins against her open lips, gasped for air at the same time. He couldn't turn his head, the pressure from above was too strong, and slowly the darkness that surrounded his eyes became bright. Primo traveled though his life, and the familiar faces flashed in front him. His wild movements were not necessarily misunderstood, because he didn't try to really free himself. Then he fell back, and all around him it was still.

Maria, overwhelmed by Primo's eruption, rose up one more time, pushed down even harder on his face, and her whole body spasmed and shuddered.

The night watchman, who was making his rounds on the second floor, heard the loud, shrill cry of a woman. He ran to the staircase, up to the third floor to the Children's Department and shined his flashlight into the dark corridors. In the stuffed animal section, he saw a half-naked woman sitting on the stomach of a huge, fallen teddy bear. The head of a man was in her lap. Except for his undershirt, he didn't have anything on, and seemed to be asleep.

"Primo, wake up, please wake up!" The woman sobbed and repeated the phrase over and over again.

But Primo didn't move. He was finally home. ▪

The Holiday

WE WERE THREE FAMILIES who wanted to go on holiday together. It was a stupid idea. It wouldn't work. We were three men and three women, with seven children between the ages of two and ten.

Robert took on the task of finding a house. In the *Frankfurter Allgemeinen*, he found an ad by a Greek architect married to a German who had a rental house available for the summer on Hydra, a small island not far from Athens. Robert wrote a letter to the owner, who sent back a form, and following payment of half the rental fee we had ourselves a summer home.

Otto, the third family man, had met Robert many years earlier while on holiday in Majorca. Robert had been working during the summer at a steel plant in the Ruhr area, and, after he had spent two months determining the lime content of the blast furnaces' cooling water, he went to a travel agency and booked the cheapest holiday available with the money he had left. That's how he got to Majorca.

Robert told me later that he had been sitting on a small towel on the hot sand, bored to tears on the crowded beach. Otto spoke to him, because he, too, didn't know what he was supposed to be doing there. Otto had not originally intended to go to Majorca. He lived in northern Germany near the Dutch border. He had inherited a third of a timber factory from his parents, which he ran together with a representative of the other shareholders, even though he had stressed again and again during his time as an anti-capitalist, anti-establishment student in Hamburg that he would never take on his father's inheritance. He had planned a trip with his mother to Romania but had confused the day of departure. When they came to the airport on the wrong day, the travel agent offered them Spain as an alternative, since a plane was ready for takeoff and had a few empty seats. The hotel in Majorca was so horrible that Otto's mother preferred to admit herself into a private clinic in the capital complaining of a bout of rheumatism. There, she had a lovely room with view of a park, and even the food was wonderful.

At that time, Otto often spoke to Robert of a new girl-friend he had met in Hamburg, and showed Robert a picture of her. Her name was Grete, and she was a small, chubby-cheeked blonde woman with cheerful eyes. The two got married later, and together with their children, the six-year old Stefan and the ten-year old Sonja, came with us to Greece.

In essence, I was only friends with Robert. Not Otto, not Grete, not the children, and I wasn't interested in Tanja, Robert's girlfriend, either. I wanted to hang out with Robert. The three-family vacation seemed like a good occasion to make tolerable the horrors of the inevitable annual family summer vacation by whiling away the hours with Robert.

I was living with Anna at the time. We were not married, despite the two children we had. Anna was a year older than I was and came from a small village located in the south of Austria near the Italian border. Her father was a small, wiry man with a wrinkled face, forever weathered by the wind and sun, who had worked all his life at a power plant in a nearby town and would thoughtfully hide *The National* newspaper in a drawer before I came to visit.

Anna often told me about the harsh upbringing of her father, who had to walk around in simple wooden clogs even in winter. She had never really forgiven his enthusiasm for the National Socialists, and I still don't know whether her relationship with me just wasn't an act of revenge against her parents. At the time, however, Anna was everything I had never had and had never been. Tall, slim and athletic, she had an answer for every question. Unsolvable problems caused her distress, and doubt was a sign of weakness. I think I fell in love with her when I fell asleep next to her in the car. When I woke up, we were three hundred kilometers further down the road. She held the steering wheel with both hands and smiled at me. I thought to myself that next to a woman like her you don't need to be afraid anymore.

The subject of marriage was a constant source of contention. For a while, I wanted her to convert to Judaism. She refused. She was an atheist, she told me. That doesn't matter, I'm one too, I answered.

"Then why bother?" she asked me. I couldn't explain it

to her, so everything stayed the same. I had no desire to be married by an Austrian public official.

Anna had been against this holiday with Robert and Otto from the beginning. She didn't particularly like Robert, and she didn't know Otto at all.

I arranged for my family to arrive a week later than Robert and Otto. A colleague at the hospital had fallen ill, and I had to trade my holiday with that of another physician.

Robert had been living with his German girlfriend in Berlin for two years. They had a two-year-old son. Robert's two children from his previous marriage lived in Vienna. Robert was a writer or a journalist, depending on whether you wanted to be friendly or less friendly to him. I met him during a management seminar in Wolfburg at the Volkswagen headquarters, where we both worked as facilitators for group dynamics to earn extra money.

From Vienna we had driven back to Wolfsburg in an all-terrain Mercedes that belonged to the organizer of the event. He was one of those bald-headed, tough guys who saw an adventure in every task. He raved to us that he could handle any situation on the road in any weather with his four-wheel-drive car, and he was also ready for any possible disaster.

Robert and I sat wedged in next to each other in the back seat and talked very little. After driving a few hours, Walter, the seminar organizer, talked about the work that awaited us. The participants were mainly from middle management. Working with them would not be difficult, since they were all interested in getting more training. The only problem – he was sitting in the passenger seat and turned to Robert and me as he spoke – was the period of National Socialism. Although it was directed at everyone in the car, we were five, he only looked at the two of us. Wolfsburg had a very problematic relationship to this period of German history, he went on, and it would be counterproductive to burden the participants with it.

Robert looked at me, then at Walter and said, "And what do you imagine will happen if one of us looks like a character in an editorial cartoon from the Nazi *Stürmer* newspaper?"

That's how I got to know Robert. Once you got used to his appalling remarks you found a very nice guy hiding behind them.

So we packed up our stuff in the first week in August. My two daughters, Betty and Doris, couldn't sleep out of sheer excitement the night before we left. Betty was five and Doris, seven. Betty looked like her mother and Doris more like my sister. After a two hour flight we landed in Athens, took a taxi to the port, and after a quiet ride on a hydrofoil we reached the bay of Hydra, which lay in front of us like an open book.

It was dreadfully hot that day. As the ship slowly glided towards the jetty, the white houses, which looked from afar as romantic as the ones on postcards, became dirty, dilapidated huts. I remembered the cool wind that swept around over the Semmering this time of year, and tormented myself with the same question I always asked when I went to the South: Why this heat, when in Austria it can be so pleasant during the summer?

Robert was waiting for us. I had carried the two suitcases over the narrow wooden walkway from the boat down to the wharf and was already soaking wet from the brief effort.

Robert gave us a rather cool greeting and said to me, even before Anna and the two children had caught up with us, "There's a problem. We don't have enough room."

Despite the many years we had been friends, I can't remember a moment when I hated him as much as I did then in the harbor, standing in front of him, drenched in sweat and exhausted.

"And? Where am I supposed to stay with my family?"

"We'll find something. But come inside the house first and rest."

I decided for the time being not to say anything to Anna. We dragged our luggage through the narrow streets of the port city, which teemed with crowds of tourists. Each step was a torment. As the houses became larger and the streets wider, Robert pointed to a hill that rose up behind the town, "The house is up there."

"What do you mean, up there? Do we have to carry the suitcases up there and then back down to find a hotel?" I asked him.

"What do you mean, hotel?" asked Anna. She sat on a step in front of the entrance to a small restaurant, Betty and Doris beside her, all three tired and close to tears.

"The house is too small. We can't all stay there," Robert said.

"I'm not going to take another step, you're all crazy! We spend hours flying here, then take a boat, get here totally exhausted, and now we don't even have a place to stay. I had a feeling nothing was going to work out! Damn it, I'm staying here with the kids at the restaurant. In the meantime, you can find us a new room. I don't want to live here in town anyway. We should start looking for a room somewhere on the beach."

"There is no real beach here. You have to take a boat to another bay, and there are more rocks than sand there, too." Robert grinned. He loved to get an uncertain fire really going by gently blowing on the embers.

Anna began to laugh hysterically, and yelled at me. "Wow, what a vacation! A house that is too small, and a lousy beach that is so far away it can only be reached by boat. With friends like yours, who needs enemies?" She stood up and walked with the two children to one of the plain wooden tables that were placed in the shade of the trees in front of the restaurant.

I felt too tired to argue, gave the suitcases to Anna and the children without saying a word and walked off with Robert.

"Why are you doing this to me?" I asked, but he didn't answer.

The road became steeper at the end of the village, and we walked one behind the other. I had sand in my sandals and sweat ran down my back.

"I'm not doing anything to you!" Robert said suddenly. "I have no idea how to fix this. Do you think I'm thrilled about it?"

"If I were only ... ugh, it doesn't matter.... It's my fault. Nobody can take a vacation with you, I should have known that ... maybe with you alone, but not when you come with a woman." I was talking to myself and wasn't sure if Robert could hear me.

"Come on, don't look at this as a major tragedy, and stop

thinking about all the places you'd rather be. What did you expect? You're here with a woman you haven't been able to stand for a long time, with children you'd rather only spend two hours with on Sunday afternoons, and you miss your girlfriend in Vienna. So how could it possibly be a great vacation? Think of it as a sacrifice, that this time it's not about you!"

Unfortunately, Robert was a head taller than me and stronger. If he weren't, I would certainly have tried to push him down the steep slope.

Beyond the last houses, the steep path wound in zigzags up the mountain. In the afternoon sun, the climb up became an almost unbearable task. The house lay in a hollow about half an hour above the village. It was a simple two-story stone house with a large terrace, a swimming pool and a covered outdoor dining area.

Otto sat with his wife Grete at the edge of the pool, his legs in the water, and all the children were either in or around the swimming pool. It was a beautiful picture, just the way you might imagine a holiday to be. Wet children climbed out of the water, jumped in again, threw balls or rubber rings, cheered, laughed and screamed.

At that moment I was once again optimistic that maybe we would still find a solution and could all live here.

Tom and Anita, Robert's bigger kids, got out of the water and greeted me immediately. I had known both of them for a long time, and they belonged somehow to our friendship.

Robert introduced me to his friend, Otto, whom I knew only from Robert's stories. He was a little plump, with a round face and short blond hair. "Hello! Things seem to be going well for you here," I told him.

"What? What's going on?"

"You need to speak louder, Otto has a bad ear," Robert said to me and laughed. Then he said quietly, "Don't repeat anything. He always pretends he doesn't understand, even when he's understood everything."

Even before I could greet Otto's wife, Robert pulled me into the house. On two floors there were in fact only four rooms. "Do you understand now that it won't work?" Robert asked me.

"No, I don't understand. It's hot here, we can sleep in the open air or spend the day here and go to the beach together," I suggested.

He just nodded.

"Damn it, Robert, answer me! I came here because of you –"

"Because of me? Whenever we want to see each other, we can spend two days driving to Zurich, stay in the best hotel, buy a few expensive sweaters and eat excellent food. Why bother with all the others here?"

"Now you tell me this? Now that I'm here with my family?"

I didn't want to wait for his answer, went outside, yanked off my wet shirt and pants, and jumped naked into the pool. It was wonderfully refreshing, and I calmed down a bit.

"I'll make you a proposal," I said to Robert as I dried myself off. "I'm going down now to the others, and we'll meet up for dinner at the same restaurant where Anna and the kids are. Then we can talk about everything."

Robert only nodded again. I got dressed and went back

down the steep slope. After a few minutes the cooling off period was over, and I was covered in sweat again.

I didn't even attempt to explain to Anna what had gone wrong. The whole situation was so shitty that there was nothing to discuss. At least we found a shoddy room in the back of a small inn for the first night, which could only be reached by a narrow staircase with high steps. It was under the roof, had only one sink and no shower, and to go to the toilet you had to go down the same unpleasant staircase to a lower level. The room had two bunk beds – it looked like an emergency quarters for soldiers during a training exercise.

The kids were overtired and cried all the time. They kept asking where the sea was. They had been looking forward to going to the beach and playing with the other children. Anna reminded me of her concerns about Robert's reliability and said that if the holiday was going to be spent staying here in this hole, then she would prefer to go home tomorrow.

I thought to myself that there are situations in life where you are not just punished for old sins, but are beaten to a pulp.

At nine in the evening, we all met at the restaurant. Our host pushed together several tables and retrieved from a back room these typical chairs with mesh cords for seats and hard backrests that create the worst pain in the shortest time possible.

Otto, Robert and I sat next to each other facing the three women. The children ran about among the trees and tables and came over only briefly to shove a piece of bread or meat in their mouths or to guzzle down their third or fourth bottle of Coke.

For a while we talked about the political situation at home, about the weather in Greece, about food, about everything, just not about the impossible situation of my family.

Anna was the first one who couldn't take it any longer. "So, what are we doing now?" she asked the others, but without singling anyone out.

Before even one of us could answer, Tanja, Robert's girl-friend, flew in her face. "Well, how do you think it will work? How can nine people live in that small house?"

"Then you have to crowd together a little and divide the rooms up better."

"Really, Anna? Who should I crowd together with? Maybe your boyfriend?" said Tanja, and laughed loudly.

"Why not? Something new for a change?"

"I have zero desire to swap partners – that didn't work on our last vacation," Robert interjected.

Tanja looked at him, apprehensive, because you could never tell if Robert was joking or serious.

"Why, Robert, I don't know what you expected. I thought that was great back then," Anna said to him, and Otto responded with a fit of laughter.

"I can't imagine," Tanja chimed in. "As far as I know Robert, he likes something to hold on to, not just an iron post."

"Exactly, as far as *you* know Robert. That seems to be the problem you have with him –" replied Anna.

I sat there and poked around in a fried fish but couldn't find anything but fins and bones. The conversation went on for a while, and I saw the pretty house on the hill behind the town becoming smaller and smaller until it completely disappeared from my mind.

Meanwhile, Tanja had jumped up to look for her two-year-old son, Martin. He sat at the end of a long row of tables and amused the other children by gnawing off the head of a fish and swallowing it. Over and over, Tom handed him a new fish that Martin held with one hand, took the whole head in his mouth, and simply bit it off. The children roared and shrieked with laughter.

Tanja's face was red, as it always was when she drank more than two glasses of wine. She took Martin's hand and wanted him to go with her, but he refused, and the other children didn't want this fun with the fish heads to suddenly come to an end. Martin screamed and raged, threw himself on the ground until Tanja gave in, let go of him and returned to sit with us. She looked at Robert and said, "And what about you? Are you just going to let this go on? Don't you have anything to say?"

He shook his head and laughed. Scenes like this one rather amused him.

"I'll tell you up front that if this bitch moves in with us, then I'm going home!" Tanja took the glass standing in front of Anna and gulped it down.

I suddenly felt very nauseous. I stood up, took refuge in the bathroom and threw up. When I flushed the Greek squat toilet it was so powerful the water flooded the floor and completely soaked my shoes. I was about to faint, didn't know where I should sit down, and leaned against the wall with my eyes closed.

I slowly got better. I didn't immediately go back to the others, but asked for a glass of water in the kitchen. I must have looked dreadful, because a woman from the kitchen immediately brought me a chair, a glass of water and a towel so I could wipe my sweaty face. I emptied the glass, the women took it out of my hand and brought it back filled with another drink of water. I felt how the blood rose inside my head, how it knocked and pounded against my temples. I closed my eyes for a few minutes, and everything became calm. When I opened my eyes, I saw the other women in the kitchen. Their white aprons were dirty, and they wore only thin shirts underneath them that were completely drenched in sweat. One was older, the other three, maybe her daughters, much younger. They talked constantly while they worked. The kitchen was a long narrow room with white tiles on the walls and floor that were interrupted approximately every meter by a row of blue. Several stoves covered with big black pans stood side by side against the wall. The windows were open on the opposite side to draw out the smoke. The elderly woman constantly stirred the food in the pots and pans that were sitting on the flames, every now and then tasted her cooking with a big ladle, and poured water in the pans afterwards. In the middle of the kitchen was a long table where the other three women worked. It was covered with vegetables, potatoes, bowls of cooked rice and ground meat.

One of the younger girls – she was tall and strong, her dark hair tied in a knot – cut a slice from each tomato, dug the seeds out of the fruit and handed the portions to the next girl, who filled them with a mixture of rice and meat. The third was the youngest and had, in contrast to the others, dark blonde hair that fell in her eyes. She repeatedly pushed her hair away with the back of her hand, had a massive, long face with a large, straight nose and a full lower lip, sucked air in through her nose, and her whole torso and her large, firm breasts heaved like mountains of pudding. She stood somewhat to one side, turned a meat grinder with a hand crank, and crammed chopped chunks of meat into the funnel. She never looked at where she was pushing in the meat, and I was afraid she would hurt her fingers. But her every move was like the movement of the gears in a clock that had been turning for centuries to the same rhythm.

Due to fatigue and exhaustion, my imagination raced around the room. I saw myself at the side of these magnificent women in this kitchen far away from Vienna, from the hospital, my family and lost friends. Living here seemed to be the only reality and the only worthwhile thing. This life had order, the children took over the work of the parents, married someone from the village, had children who perpetuated these cycles. None of these three young women would ever feel estranged here, they would never be different; no one would ever see them as different.

I knew that in this house there was a closet where the shoes of their grandfather were kept and their grandmother's wedding dress. The family could build something and pass it on to their kids. They had everything here I never did, and I had always missed it.

"Ah, here you are – I was looking everywhere for you!" Anna screamed at me. "The others are gone, your good friends – They just left!"

"Robert, too?" I asked.

"Yes, even your best friend Robert! Off to the fine little house on the hill, maybe even a little swim before bed, and admiring the stars through an open window while lying in bed with a lover. And tomorrow morning, the magnificent sunrise over the bay. What a divine, splendid life we have here!"

I was not angry with her because of her bad mood, but I was angry because she had brought me back to my crummy little life while I was in search of happiness on, of all places, a Greek island.

We went to our awful room but were so exhausted the awfulness didn't even bother us, and we immediately crawled into bed. I lay awake for a long time while everyone slept, and thought about the last few hours. My stomach convulsed with cramps, and I constantly had the feeling I needed to go to the toilet.

The next morning I went to a pharmacy, showed the owner my doctor's identification, and bought a pack of anticonvulsant suppositories. With this I intended to survive the day. Back in the room I pushed an overdose of this agent up my back end and decided to make the most of the time here. The remedy acted in almost no time; I felt as if my arms and legs were moving like a puppet's.

We packed our bathing suits in a plastic bag and went to the harbor where small motorboats waited to take tourists to the beach. After about twenty minutes on a rickety boat, we came to a bay with a narrow, stony beach and a few trees, whose small shady areas were already occupied by other bathers. I saw Robert and the others under a tree and we went up to them.

The mood was unbearable. No one spoke a word. The women played with exaggerated cheerfulness with the children, Robert and Otto lay far apart from one another, each buried in a book and lying on his own towel. On the last narrow strip of shade, I spread a blanket we had brought along, lay on my back and fell asleep immediately, thanks to the suppository that was still poisoning my body.

I don't know how long I slept, but when I was awakened by the loud shrieks of a woman, the shade had long since moved and I was lying in the blazing sun. My head was heavy, and for a moment I didn't know where I was until I recognized the voice that had awakened me. It was Tanja, Robert's girlfriend.

"He's drowning – This idiot – He's going to kill himself! All because of this stupid dispute here! Nothing but children – No Men – They are children!"

She ran up and down the beach and kept looking at the sea. Otto and Grete stood beside her and tried to calm her. My children and Anna were nowhere in sight.

Still dazed by the sun, I got up, staggered to the water and jumped through a high wave coming toward me. After a few strokes I crawled back out of the water on all fours, so I wouldn't be flipped over by the breaking waves. Tanja was still pacing nervously, tears in her eyes, her gaze fixed somewhere out on the sea.

"What's the matter?" I asked her.

"You'd better hold your tongue, everything that's happened is your fault!" she snapped at me.

I had no idea what had happened, and looked at the sea like the others. In the distance was a small island. It jutted from the water, and at its highest point one could see a small chapel.

"Robert has swum to the island," Otto said softly, almost in a whisper, as if it were a secret.

"So, what's the problem?" I asked.

"What's the problem? You idiot! He'll never make it – That's crazy, completely crazy!" Tanja began again with this screeching sound I could not bear.

"So what? If he doesn't make it, what's the problem?"

The effect of the suppository was phenomenal. All my despair was gone, and all the rage I had been carrying around since our arrival on this damned island found expression.

Tanja was so taken aback by my answer that she didn't respond. I saw my chance and flew into a rage.

"It's my fault, isn't it? Yes, it's as simple as that, you fucking German cow!" I shouted at Tanja. "You hate everybody who has anything to do with Robert, his friends, his family, even his children. You come crawling to us as a German policeman's daughter, smear yourself on him to forget your shitty past, act like somebody who belongs with him, who has run away from your own home. I really have to laugh, but you will stay what you are and always have been, a German policeman's daughter, and nothing else, nothing...! You can destroy, yes, you do that brilliantly. Destroy friendships, destroy the holidays of others, smash and destroy – Bravo! You can be proud – You did it!"

Tanja put her arms on her hips and struck back. "Ah, now the little one plays the Jewish card – Barely separated from the bottle, he starts in on the evil Germans, great! Yes, it was me, of course, I took away the poor little boy's favorite toy, his friend. Oh God, oh God, the wicked women, the evil Germans, the terrible evil German women – The two little ones can't play together anymore in the sandbox. And why not? It's the evil German women again!"

We didn't spare each other. Each of us sang our aria with such virtuosity that it became a spectacle for everyone else who, rather intimidated, witnessed the duel. I made Tanja out to be a perfect member of the Nazi League of German Girls and saw her with a white blouse and two blonde pigtails, and for her I was the lousy, evil Jew with crooked nose and a black, dirty caftan.

We were about to rip into each other again when Otto interrupted us. "Hey look, now – There on the island, I think it's Robert –"

Next to the small church on the summit of the hill on the island stood a man who was waving both arms. We didn't hear his voice, but tried to call out to him and shouted loudly.

At that moment Anna arrived with the children and asked what had happened, why everyone was yelling and shouting, and immediately it started up again between Anna and Tanja. It was unbearable. Even my suppository could not compensate for this level of anger, hatred and disgust.

I decided to follow Robert's lead, took my straw hat and walked slowly away from the group so that nobody noticed. A few hundred meters away I could still hear them as they tried to shout to Robert, or to yell at each other.

At the end of the bay was a small pine forest. A path led through the trees. The needles stung me – I had, in my hurry, forgotten my shoes. I went over a small hill, and when I came out of the woods, I saw the next bay. It was a bit smaller but just as stony as the other one and had even fewer trees. At the end of the bay, I could see a small tavern. I was thrilled. That was exactly what I was looking for, a shady place, a glass of cold water, a strong coffee, and as far as the eye could see, nobody, no friends, no enemies, no family.

I ran in high spirits down the hill to the beach and to the tavern. A few tables and chairs were set up in front of a simple house made of rough, heavy stones. The withered branches that wove around the wooden arbor over the tables provided little shade.

One of the tables stood against the wall. It was the only place where the sun no longer reached. A man sat at the table, in front of him a small bronze coffee pot, a white cup and a glass of water. As I got closer, I recognized Robert.

I walked up to him and was not sure whether this conversation might mean the end of our friendship. But when I stood in front of him, he said, with that damned smirk on his face, "And where have you been? How much longer am I supposed to wait for you?" ∎

The Aunt

I T HAPPENED on a Sunday morning in May. The beginning of May. I don't know the exact day anymore. That can be determined. It was 10:30 in the morning, and I was already half an hour late.

"Hey! Where are we going?"

The nurse stood in front of me the same as last Sunday and the Sunday before that. She must work the night shift. Did she ever have Sunday off? I had run up the two flights of stairs, taking two steps at a time.

"I have to go see my aunt –" I gasped and couldn't breathe.

"So he wants to go see his aunt, does he? And what is his aunt's name?"

She had a broad face, and everything about her was big: eyes, lips, even her ears, and of course, her breasts. "My aunt Martha, Martha Wiener, Room 16. You know me – This is the second floor?"

"So he would like to go see his Aunt Martha, would he? Such a nice boy. And the flowers are probably for her?"

I took a step back. My eyes wandered slowly from her

short blonde hair down to her legs, which stuck out from under a white, buttoned coat. You could see her firm round knees. Damned beautiful woman. Too young, too beautiful and too naughty for a retirement home. When she grinned, her mouth opened so wide that you could slide a slice of bread between her teeth.

"You're the nephew, aren't you? Your name's Jurek?"

"Yes, I am. We've seen each other many times, but how come you know my name? Does she talk about me sometimes?"

"Of course, every day. Your aunt loves you as much as it's possible to love someone."

The way she said that: Love! It was like in a TV movie.

"That's nice. Who loves anybody these days anymore?"

She stood in front of me, and we didn't know what we should do. Every Sunday we exchanged a few words and went our separate ways. A few times I was thinking about asking her out or something, but it had never happened.

For a while neither of us moved. One of us would have to take the first step. She looked into my eyes, and I felt she had caught me thinking the dirtiest thoughts. Then she took my arm. "Come on – Your aunt's not there now, she's with a doctor."

"What's wrong with her?"

"Nothing special. She can't sleep, just like everyone else here. You can wait with me for now."

She grabbed me by the arm and pushed me across the aisle to her room. These were simple quarters with a table, a few chairs and those typical cabinets with glass doors where you can see boxes of medications. In one corner was a bed with a gray blanket and a white pillow.

"Sit down –"

I pulled a chair away from the table and sat down. "How is my aunt?"

"Just fine. Better than most here. She can at least go to the bathroom by herself and doesn't have to go in her bed –"

She laughed and leaned back against the closet, folded her arms and pressed them against her upper body, so that its two hemispheres almost fell out of her dress. The bottom and top buttons of her dress were undone.

I didn't know where I should look.

"What's your first name?" I asked.

"Lena."

"Nice name. Doesn't sound Viennese."

"My mother comes from Prague, my father is from here."

"Like me."

"Well, well, then we have something in common –" She walked slowly over to me and sat on my knee. Light, she was not.

"What is this all about?" I asked her.

"Whatever you want it to be about."

I began to sweat, felt how my face flushed, let my arms hang down at the sides, and tried not to look into the opening of her dress. But I didn't succeed.

"Have a look!"

"And if someone comes?"

She got up, walked slowly to the door and locked it. "So now there's no more going back. Hurry, you have five minutes."

"I can't, not in five minutes!"

"Ha!" She laughed out loud. "What is that supposed to mean? What can't you do?"

"Yes, I'm sorry." I started to stutter. "For me, it takes too long. I'm not like one of those fast – how shall I put it? – hart, no stag deer, maybe. I'm something like half capable."

She laughed again. "I don't buy it, not with your looks – You can have any woman!"

"Yes, that's just my problem. I can have them, but then it doesn't work the way they imagine, it doesn't work."

"You can't tell me that. Nobody has ever had a problem with me –"

She walked up to me and slowly unbuttoned her white dress. A row of buttons ran down the front. There was a tight bra under it and a pair of black panties that were visible through the white work dress.

I stared. "Why do you wear white on top and black on the bottom?"

"Above, I'm an angel, but down there, a devil!"

"Why aren't you in the movies?"

She laughed again and took my hand the way my mother did when we were crossing the street, and pushed me down on the bed with both hands and pulled off my sweater, opened my belt, then the button, pulled the zipper down and pulled my pants and underwear together down to the knees. I simply closed my eyes and waited.

"Hey! That looks like an elephant's trunk. You're not circumcised – I thought you weren't supposed to have a foreskin."

"What? Oh you mean...? How do you know that?"

"Well, from that aunt of yours?"

I sat up and said what I always say in these situations. "I'm circumcised, but it wasn't done quite right. The rabbi was drunk and messed up –"

"Well, thank God he cut off too little and not too much –"

She laughed, and again she opened her big mouth. I tried to kiss her, but it was hard. Her mouth was just too big. I felt her teeth and pulled back. She didn't close her mouth, and I was afraid she would bite down.

"Hey, you can do something after all –"

She kissed me on the face, licked my cheeks, ears and neck. Everything was moist. Then she got interested in my penis again. She pulled the foreskin all the way back. "It should be that far back, and the head should be uncovered –"

"Yes, it should be, but it's not. Yet, it's not like the others. Look – If you compare it to others a piece is missing."

"Yes, you're right again."

She moved the skin back and forth. Then she reached between my legs and took my balls in her hand like a couple of hard boiled eggs and rolled them around back and forth and stroked my penis at the same time.

"You're right. Nothing going on here –"

"I told you so –"

But she would not give up so easily. She knelt on the floor, pulled the shortened foreskin back completely and began to kiss my cock. Then she swallowed it. It disappeared completely in her mouth.

"There you go! Something's happening –"

"That doesn't mean a thing. I never come –"

I leaned back and closed my eyes. Lena was excited because of my slow arousal and worked intensely on my cock. I don't know how she did it, but the simultaneous effect of lips and hands woke even my organ, and it condescended to release a few drops after the lengthy treatment.

I moaned and groaned and whipped back and forth, grabbing her hair and reached for her breasts.

"Well?"

"Unbelievable. This hasn't happened to me in years –"

"Really? That's great, I didn't know I'm so good –"

"Yes, you are!"

"Come on, scoot over."

Then she lay down beside me and burrowed her head in my armpit. I wanted to ask if I should help her somehow, but after a few seconds I heard her snoring. She had fallen asleep.

I didn't move and looked at the room. Above the table hung a wooden cross, underneath it a board covered with postcards. Beaches, nothing but empty beaches. On the table, an electric coffee maker and a couple of cups. There was a name on each one, Lena among them, then Anna, Josephine and Susanne. On another wall hung a calendar with a photo from the Semmering. On display next to it a roster, with red circles around different dates.

We lay together for only a few minutes. Then Lena moved, stretched her legs and opened her eyes. "Oh –" She sighed. "That was wonderful –" She kissed me on the cheek.

I wanted to ask something but didn't know what. It probably would have been the usual questions, whether now she wanted something, or some other bullshit full of guilty feelings and complexes.

But she just stood up, straightened her dress and opened the door. I slipped out, wanted to kiss her again, but she turned away.

"Go on, your aunt is waiting –"

My aunt's room was just a few doors down. A man in a wheelchair sat in front of the nurses' station in the corridor. He grinned at me. A few individual teeth remained in the center of his mouth. They were black. His head was bald, and a few tubes came from his neck and ended in a plastic bag. A cloudy liquid filled the tubes. His hands on the armrests of his chair trembled constantly and caused the plastic bag to swing back and forth.

He looked like death, but he smiled as if he knew exactly what had played out behind the door. He tried to say something, leaned forward and tilted his head towards me. But I didn't understand him. There was a gurgle and a cough; he made an effort, his face turned red, and his bald head began to glow. He coughed and choked, tried to swallow, his trembling got worse.

"There, there, Mr. Martin –"

Lena came out and took care of the man. She pushed him back into his chair and stroked his head. He calmed down. When she wheeled him away, he kept trying to turn around and look at me as though he wanted to tell me something else.

I went to my aunt's room. She was sitting in a wheelchair next to the bed. A blanket lay over her legs. Another woman was in the second bed in the room, sitting upright with a couple of big pillows behind her back. I had never seen her before. I smiled, and she smiled back. She had a narrow, fine, almost youthful face. Under her colorful dressing gown I could see the peaks of an expensive nightgown. She had to be older than Aunt Martha, I thought, and maybe once a fine lady.

"Where were you so long?" Martha coughed.

"I was waiting outside until you came back from the doctor. I've been here a long time."

"What are you talking about, I wasn't with a doctor –"

"I thought..."

"Oh – You and your excuses!"

I looked at the other woman. She nodded and smiled.

"Let's go!" Martha was looking for something under the blanket on her lap.

Then her fingers froze. She seemed to have found it. I pushed the wheelchair out of the room.

When I was in the doorway, the other woman cried: "Young man –"

She had a whispery voice that could barely be heard.

I stopped and turned around. "What?"

Martha was annoyed.

"That woman there, I think she wants something –"

"Leave her alone – She's crazy!"

"Young man!" cried the woman again.

I pushed the wheelchair down the hallway and went back to her bed.

"My name is Anna Berger, and someone is going to kill me! Your aunt has ordered it –" She whispered and smiled.

I nodded and took her hand. "They will take good care of you here."

Martha got angry outside in the hallway. She banged her hand against her wheelchair and yelled to come on already and leave the crazy old woman in peace.

The old woman pulled herself up on my arm close to my face. "They are going to kill me – Your aunt wants it that way –"

"I don't believe that –" I knew it was the wrong answer,

but it didn't seem to bother her. Then I laid her back on her many cushions, went out to Aunt Martha and pushed her wheelchair down the hallway.

"Did she tell you that somebody is going to kill her? This crazy old cow! Fifty years ago she was the great heroine, and now she trembles before me. Why did they put me in a room with her? And why don't I have a single room? Old Wertheim, never worked a day in her whole life, but she got a single room on the first floor – With a balcony! Pospisyl, an old fool, but a single room for her. Novotny complains all day to her children, they pay for her single room. But not for me – I have to share a room with an old Nazi!"

I didn't answer her. I knew what was coming, it was repeated every Sunday. She had no husband, no children, no money, was always left alone, had enjoyed life; and now there was nothing left. And most of all, there was no one who could support her now.

"Why can't you afford more things? You will soon be forty, and you still haven't made a good life for yourself –"

"Obviously, I'm a loser –"

"Ridiculous, an excuse. Good that your blessed mother can't hear you –"

I took the elevator down to the ground floor. A young woman stood next to me. She had long blonde hair, a black sweater and tight black pants. Her ass was too big and her pants too small so that they rode up into her crotch. An old man sat in a wheelchair in front of her. He was asleep. His head had slipped to one side, and snot ran out of his nose. Maybe he wasn't even alive anymore. The young woman tried to wipe the snot, but more kept running out his nose.

Martha put her hands over her eyes and turned away. The young woman looked at me, shrugged and rolled her eyes. I grinned. She looked at Martha and smiled.

I pushed the wheelchair onto the gravel road through the park. The sun was warm, people began to undress slowly, took off their winter clothes, opened their jackets and blouses. Their bodies seeking the sun.

"Stop there, nobody can see me there." Martha pointed to a large, dense shrub. She always wanted to hide behind the same shrubbery every Sunday. I pushed her over the meadow behind this wall of green and sat down on the grass. Martha reached under the blanket that was folded over her knees, and retrieved a pack of cigarettes and a lighter. Her fingers trembled as she took a cigarette out and tried to light it.

"So help me, already!"

The lighter didn't work. She shook it furiously. It slipped out of her hand and flew off in a high arc.

Martha became nervous. She simply needed the cigarette. "Go get it!" she yelled, and her voice had this hysterical high pitch.

I crawled around on all fours and looked for the lighter in the grass.

"What are you doing?"

Lena was standing in front of me. This time she was all buttoned up. She wasn't smiling, either.

"You again – I'm looking for something –"

"Jurek – What is it?" shouted Martha from behind the shrub. Lena went back and saw my aunt sitting in her wheelchair with the shaky cigarette in her hand. "Now, now, Mrs. Wiener, we don't like to see this." She took her cigarette from her fingers, crumbled it up and threw it on the ground. "And you shouldn't bring such a thing to her, Rascal!" She threatened with a finger, came very close to my face, smiled again, turned around and left.

I found the lighter.

Martha took another cigarette from under the blanket. "Come on, Give me a light already!"

I looked around. Lena was nowhere to be seen. I pushed down the lighter; it worked. Martha sucked in the smoke. Her face acquired a peaceful expression. She leaned back, stretched out her legs and wiggled her toes. "This feels good. Don't you want one, too?"

"You know I don't smoke –"

"What appeals to you? Tell me, what you like to do for fun? You always have such a miserable expression –"

I scratched my chin and ran my hand over my close-cropped hair. "Well, that's not so easy to answer."

"You married a woman you don't love. It would be enough for you to see your children once a week, your job lets you get by, but there's no real money in it. What is wrong with you?"

I shrugged. "It's not so bad. Was your life always so great?"

"Pha!" She laughed out loud. "You have no idea – Men, you know, men were always hitting on me. They shaped my life."

"Then why didn't you ever get married?"

"I loved these goy men with their broad shoulders and their direct ways. They didn't talk so much and worked hard. But marry one of them? How can one marry such animals? I'm not getting married to a horse just because it's great at galloping through the forest –"

"Come on, it's getting cool, we need to go back."

Martha held the butt with her fingertips and almost burned her lips on the last draw. Then she flicked the butt in the grass and fished out the next cigarette. "One more. The last one!"

"I have to go, Martha."

"Really? Where? Back to your wife, maybe?"

"Leave her out of this, what has she ever done to you? I'll take you back to your room."

"You don't allow me anything."

I pushed her slowly down the path, gravel blocked the wheels and the wheelchair jerked and kept getting stuck. Old men and women came to meet us, greeted us, and Martha had a story about every one of them.

It had become midday. Visitors crowded into the retirement home, arms full of flowers and gifts. Small children ran around in front of the house on the lawn while their parents tried to be kind to their fathers and mothers, at least for an hour. The same questions were asked as last Sunday, and they prompted the same answers.

I pushed Martha through the visitors and the visited, heard the laughter of children and the coughing of the sick. Martha, my mother's sister, was my last family. Mother dead, father dead, grandparents I never met, and the many uncles and aunts I only knew from old photographs. Every week, I looked forward to the visit, and when I was there, I didn't know what I should talk to her about. I made up my mind every time to ask her about the past, people I had never known, the many relatives that I had never seen, but it never came about.

Martha wanted to smoke and nothing else would do. Sometimes we went to a restaurant. There she ate so fast and so much she felt sick, then we went back to the home.

"Hurry, turn somewhere, don't stop," Martha said suddenly and seemed to shrink in her wheelchair.

A man came to meet us, upright, no cane, thick white hair, dark suit, red tie and matching handkerchief.

"Mrs. Wiener, how nice to see you here!" he exclaimed from afar and came towards us.

"I told you –" she hissed at me, but then her voice turned friendly, sweet. "Doctor – How wonderful! How are you?"

He stood next to the wheelchair, one hand on her shoulder, and beamed at her. Up close, he didn't look so great. He had scaly patches on his neck, white shimmering round pieces of skin that flaked off. His hands were covered with them.

"May I introduce myself? Dr. Steiner. Incidentally, not contagious –" He stretched out his hand. I took it as gingerly as though it were the handle of a hot pan and let it go again immediately.

"Yes, it is nice to see you again, but I must get back right away. Unfortunately, the bladder, you know, at my age." Martha turned and looked at me sternly. "Go on! By the way, Jurek Galinski, my nephew. My last relative, unfortunately, a loser, but at least he comes every Sunday."

The doctor laughed and said goodbye. I pushed the wheelchair along.

"Lousy old Nazi! He was in the SS for many years and now he creeps after me as if I could help him restore his innocence. Who am I? His confessor? Tells me how many Jewish friends he had before the war and after the war.

And how much he helped in the time in between. What is he thinking? Why should I care? Why does everybody think they have to talk to me about Jews and persecution? Jurek, why do you still live here? Why don't you leave this country?"

Now we would start that again.

"Why did you come back?" I asked in response.

She didn't answer.

"Why have you lived here for years, and why didn't you stay in London?"

"You don't understand –"

"That's an answer?"

"What would I do in London? Listen to the Bronner on a CD? Spend every afternoon in the only Viennese pastry shop across from Harrod's? Play cards with the old emigrants and dream of the past? I wanted to live! And you can only live at home, even if it's difficult –"

"And I, why shouldn't I stay here?"

"Pha!" She laughed. "You call this life?"

"You came back here with my parents – It was your decision, not mine. I grew up here. You all made me a Viennese Jew!"

"Viennese Jew? What kind of Viennese Jew are you? There haven't been any Viennese Jews since the Anschluss. Your generation whines so loudly, you have forgotten to live – You live more in the past than I do. And the old Eastern Jews have been sitting around in temple for fifty years, using language like a coachman from Timisoara –"

"There's no point in talking about this; it always makes you angry."

"Yes, I'm angry at you! Wake up, little one – Take what is

not yours, and don't wait for them to hand it to you – They will never give you anything voluntarily –"

"Who?"

"Everybody! Even if they treat us like a dying animal species –"

"You're probably right."

We entered the home, and I pushed her to the dining room.

"Take me back to my room, I want to eat alone today."

Even this was repeated every Sunday. It meant that I would remain with her until she finished her meal.

Mrs. Berger was in the room. She had ordered her lunch in, too.

"She's still here –" Martha whispered.

"Leave her alone –"

I called the nurse's station and asked for lunch.

Mrs. Berger was sitting on a chair that was attached to a table. The small wooden platform was fastened to the chair by an iron rod that bent up from the base. On it stood a tray with lunch.

There was a knock, and Lena came in. She pushed in a new chair with a table – lunch was already on it. "And the kid? Does he want anything?"

"The kid?" Martha laughed. "He was never a kid. Even as a child he had a face full of worry lines."

Lena looked at me with her big eyes, and I wanted nothing more than to return to her room, under her white coat. Both of us helped Martha into the dining chair.

Mrs. Berger began to cough. She couldn't stop. Her face became red. Lena struck her gently on the back, then increasingly harder, but it was no use. Mrs. Berger wheezed and rasped, could not breathe, and Lena yelled at me to get in the hallway and look for the doctor.

Then Mrs. Berger cried one last time, it was more of a grunt, and a large piece of chicken fell from her mouth back into the plate. After that, came the rice, the vegetables and at last the soup. She stopped coughing.

"I feel better now," said Ms. Berger and wiped her face with a napkin. Lena lifted her from the chair, helped her into bed and covered her up. Mrs. Berger lay back and closed her eyes.

"Rest for a while, I'll clean this first, then I will come back."

Lena pushed Mrs. Berger's dining chair slowly out of the room. The tray was full of vomit, and Lena tried to keep anything from spilling on the floor.

"You can pick up my lunch, too!" Martha called to her. Then to me, "Go on – Take me to the dining room –"

"And the woman here? Should we leave her alone?" I asked.

"Let her croak, the old sow. What did she ever do for me back then? Come on, get me out of here!" ■

Onju

T HE RABBI WAS a young man, not yet forty, not big, not small, with a round, heavy belly that hung over his belt. At least one button on his tight-fitting white shirt was always open. His black hat was too small, his beard thin and, despite his youth, it was sprinkled with a number of gray hairs.

One could call him neither a handsome nor even a dignified man. He lacked the charisma of a wise man, his voice was light and thin, and his words came haltingly. What he said was often difficult to understand. He jumped from one topic to another and lost the thread of his discourses, so that he ended on a different subject than he had intended at the beginning of the conversation.

Still, everyone loved him. Despite all his faults, he exuded humanity and goodness, so that everyone liked to approach him with their problems and only very rarely left him without feeling a sense of relief. As much as he lacked the ability to captivate larger audiences, so much more was it possible for him to provide comfort in private conversation, to help or cheer up a desperate man so that his almost insoluble problem seemed small, insignificant and no longer unmanageable.

He had his office hours every morning between ten and twelve o'clock. He waited for his visitors in a small room on the second floor of an office building that was right next to the synagogue. It was rare that the rabbi received visitors at other times, but it was possible. One could telephone him at home and get an appointment before or after a wedding, a funeral or a circumcision. Even if he only had a few minutes, it was more important to the rabbi to listen to the concerns of the petitioners than to dismiss them.

One day the rabbi got a call that was different than the many daily others he received. It was a male voice that was familiar to him, but he couldn't recall the face that it belonged to. It was the voice of an old man who asked the rabbi if he could speak with him. The rabbi pointed out his office hours, as he often did in such cases, but the old man declined and said that it was impossible for him to come to the temple's office; they must meet at a different place. The rabbi had answered the call on a wintery Friday afternoon. The sun did not intend to shine upon the city much longer, and the time was approaching when the faithful among the Jews began to prepare for the Sabbath. The rabbi, who otherwise patiently lent his ear to each petitioner, had to break off the conversation and say to the old man that rather than being entirely alone with his worries, he could come to the temple for the service.

It was a cold night, and the rabbi went alone to the synagogue this time. His six-year-old son, who always accompanied him, had a fever and was not allowed to leave his bed.

The way to the temple took at most ten minutes, but this time the wind blew icy cold in his face. He was constantly afraid of losing his hat, and he probably wouldn't make it there even in double the usual time. He crept close to the house walls, crossed the old University Square, walked through the doorway of a building and out the back of it to take a shortcut.

It was the same path that his father had taken before him, who had been a rabbi for many years in the same city.

Only a few had come to the synagogue, a few older men and women. The mood was not cheerful and there was no joyful expectation in this hour before the start of the Sabbath. The rabbi was actually glad when it was over; he longed for the hot soup and cooked chicken that awaited him at home.

He was the last one to walk to the door; the others tried to reach their homes or cars that were parked at a considerable distance as quickly as possible. The rabbi turned up his coat collar, pulled the scarf almost to his eyes and was about to leave when someone touched him on the shoulder. He turned around and saw an old, emaciated man in an expensive coat, its inner fur lining sticking out at the collar, wearing a fur cap on his head that the rabbi had otherwise only seen on actors in American Westerns.

"Excuse me, you're the rabbi?" the old man asked timidly.

"Yes, what is it?"

"I called you this afternoon."

The rabbi recognized the voice and also the man's face. "I know you, you were once in our temple and donated the Sabbath meal."

The man nodded.

"I can't help you just now, my family is waiting at home, you should know ..."

"Only ten minutes, I beg you, only ten minutes." The old man clapped his hands together.

"How do you think that would work, where would we go? I need to go home now, and it is too cold to be standing around in the street. Why don't you come to the temple tomorrow morning, we'll have plenty of time then."

"No, I can't go to the temple any longer. Now - It must be now, I don't know what I will do until tomorrow."

"All right." The rabbi was not enthusiastic about his own idea, but what else could he do now? He invited the stranger to accompany him home.

"I'll be satisfied if I can walk with you to your front door."

They walked a few steps next to each other without speaking. The rabbi interrupted the silence, "What is your name?"

"Slansky, Harry Slansky."

"Oh, now I remember. You came back with the family from the United States."

"Yes, I have lived there since the end of the war and wanted to return to Vienna. My daughter, her husband and her son came with me."

"You must speak louder, I can hardly hear you." The rabbi leaned over to the old man and almost shouted in his face.

The man stopped and took an envelope from his coat pocket. "I've brought you this letter. I think you're not allowed to open it tonight. Also, there is no money in the envelope. It's not sealed, I just want you to read the letter."

"Now? Here, in the street? How am I supposed to do that?"

"Read it, I beg you, read it."

"No, I can't take it and just read it here, you know that."

"Fine, then I will read it to you. I won't let myself be stopped by any law."

The rabbi felt edgy. This was not an ideal way to start the Sabbath. His family waiting at home, his son sick in bed, his wife in the kitchen in front of the hot food, the table set. He was at least able to calm the old man enough to keep him from reading the letter in the middle of the sidewalk.

They reached the entrance of the house where the rabbi lived, pushed the heavy iron door open and stood in the hallway, when Slansky said, "I won't go up with you. Just stay a few minutes, and I'll read this letter to you."

There was no way to escape now. The two stood facing each other in their heavy coats. Slansky took the envelope from his pocket and removed the letter. It was handwritten with blue ink.

"Will you tell me who the letter is from and what it's about?"

"It's written by a girl, her name is Sonja. The letter is addressed to her boyfriend, Robert. Robert is my grandson. Both are seventeen years old and go to the same school."

"How did you get the letter?"

"I found it by accident. I know I should not have taken it, I know. You're always right, but please listen to me, then you'll know why."

The rabbi leaned against the wall, unbuttoned his coat, took the scarf off his neck and the hat from his head, and Slansky began to read.

My dear Robert –

I've been working for days on this letter. Not writing it, but working on it. Every afternoon after school, in the evenings, and often late into the night. I was planning to explain to you why I can't see you anymore, why I can't laugh like before when we are together, why I am scared by the thought of a touch from you, where before we used to have such a nice time together.

I can't explain any of it to you. But eventually I had to recognize that I can't give you a logical justification. I can only tell you what I've experienced in the last three weeks and how much it's affected me.

I don't know whether you can understand me. This sounds very cold, but don't be angry, because I don't care how you will respond to this letter. I must write it, maybe more for me than for you.

It all started three weeks ago, when I accompanied my grandmother to temple on Sunday morning. You know her from your visits with us. She is a grumpy woman but still lovely. Leave me alone, I can walk on my own, she said then, angrily, when I tried to help her. She propped herself up with her right hand on a cane and pushed me away with her sharp elbow. Have I fallen down yet? Then you can help me, but now I want to walk on my own! Slowly, with small, careful steps she drew near the entrance of the synagogue. The street was wet from snow that had fallen on the town the night before and melted again in the morning. It was one of those gray mornings, not winter, not spring, not really cold anymore and not yet warm.

Two young men stood in front of the entrance of the synagogue. When grandmother approached the door, one of them stepped in front of her with his arms crossed. Do you have an ID card? he asked with a Slavic accent.

What do you want from me, a card? You snot-nosed brat, you are asking for a pass from me? Her legs began to tremble, and she sought my arm with her left hand. I tried to calm her and told her the two young men were only doing their duty. You are defending them, these lousy bastards? she yelled at me. They can ID whomever they want, but me? How many decades have I gone into this temple, every Saturday, every Friday evening? And now these two, who can't even speak German, want to see a pass. We've come a long way – Am I glad that your righteous grandfather did not live to see this! Then she pushed one of the two men aside, who stepped back startled.

The other, however, stepped in front of her and snapped: No ID, no entry, new rules.

Sonja – Let's go! she said to me. I don't have a temple in this town anymore. It's time for me to wait for the Messiah in a different place. Grandmother turned and began to go laboriously back down the steep path.

But then the door of the temple opened and the rabbi stepped out. Mrs. Wagner! he cried, Come in, where are you going?

She stopped and looked the rabbi, who had followed her, in the eye. He was startled by her tears and offered her his arm. She took it, and together they went back to the entrance, where with a triumphant expression she made a way for herself with her cane and didn't bother to even glance at the two men who leaned silently against the wall.

"Yes, I remember the scene," said the rabbi. He felt hot, his face was wet with sweat. He pulled off his coat, put it over his arm and nodded to Slansky.

Slansky was also leaning on the wall by now and read on:

The temple was well attended this time. In the front row sat and stood a few old men who crowded together and argued heatedly, further back sat a group of tourists with black paper yarmulkes on their heads, which they had taken from a cardboard box that was put there for visitors. With a trembling hand, the old cantor distributed books to the guests with prayers written in German on one side and Hebrew on the other. We slowly climbed up the stairs, one step after another, taking short rests as needed.

When we reached the first floor, grandmother stopped. I would like to see a temple where the men have to go upstairs and the women can sit downstairs, she said haltingly and breathed heavily. Then she walked to the fourth row from the front, where she always sat, folded down her seat, leaned her cane against the desk, sat gingerly, looked around a few times and leaned over the railing, looking for familiar and especially strange faces, which she usually found more interesting.

It was the same routine every Saturday. Grandmother showed me the important young men in the temple, who owed their importance mainly to their fathers' bank accounts. When everything was over, people could move to the back room of the temple. The cholent this time was donated by a real estate broker nobody knew. He had been in town for only a few months, it was said. No one knew where he came from, but everyone was glad he had provided for the food on Saturday and praised him for his generosity.

The beans smelled wonderful, and grandmother, who had been looking forward to the food, was among the first to stand by the pots.

When everyone was sitting around the long table, the rabbi began with the benediction, grandmother muttered impatiently, how long would she have to wait, and took the ladle so she could fill her plate first.

Then the benefactor was introduced, your grandfather, Harry Slansky, who was new to the community, had lived many years in the U.S., but now was back with his family in Vienna.

He was a small, old man with only a few hairs on his head, gray skin and thick, heavy lips that hung on him like old rags. He got up slowly, no one had noticed him before, nodded without saying a word and sat back down. Like children in a boarding school everyone grabbed at the food, piled mountains on their plates and ate like it was the night after Yom Kippur.

Pass the ladle! said a thick plump woman who was sitting next to my grandmother.

Only now I noticed that Onju was still holding the ladle in her hand. But her plate was still empty. She had put her fist on the table, the ladle in her hand sticking up into the air. Her eyes were fixed somewhere in the distance. She seemed to hear nothing, to see nothing. Then she stood up slowly, slowly put the ladle on the table and said quietly to me, Come on, Sonja, we're leaving.

But Onju, we still haven't eaten, you were looking forward to it so much, I told her.

Still in a quiet, now tortured, forced speech, she asked me to follow her. She squeezed between the chairs and the wall until she passed the rabbi who stood up and pushed his chair under the table to make room for her.

Is everything all right? he asked her.

No, it's not all right, so I'm leaving! She spoke so loudly that despite the noise in the room, everyone could hear her. It was quiet in the room now, only a few continued serving the beans and meat.

Everyone looked at her. Some covered their mouths because they had eaten too fast and tried to be as quiet as possible while they chewed the last bite.

Grandmother leaned on her cane and looked from one to the next. There were a few old men who could not look her in the eye and bowed their heads, stared at a table or a plate, as if there were something there to discover. Grandmother pointed with her cane to one of the old men, walked a few steps until she stood behind him and struck the legs of his chair with her cane. He didn't move, kept looking at his plate and didn't say a word.

Does it taste good? Then keep eating. But you won't be able to forget it, no matter how many beans you eat.

Now Slansky, the man she was standing next to, who had donated the cholent, slowly stood up, took a step back and pushed his chair in. His face was moist, beads of sweat ran down his neck to the much-too-wide shirt collar and disappeared under it. I'm sorry, I shouldn't have come, he whispered, but it was so quiet, everyone could hear him. I thought, it's all been so long.... He spoke slowly, haltingly.

But grandmother interrupted him harshly. Nothing is over, nothing and never! Then she turned to me and said, Sonja! Let's go!

We left the room and the temple and took a taxi home. Grandmother didn't observe Shabbat so well. During the ride, she didn't say one word to me.

Now, what should I have done with this experience? I had only known you for a few weeks. You came to this city like you were from another planet. Unbelievable, all that you could tell me about, all that you have experienced. I think I have said this about every new boyfriend, but with you it really was true, you were so different from the others.

Everything was beautiful with you, partly because it was so new. With the others I already knew what they were going to say as soon as they opened their mouths.

But that Sunday everything changed. I saw your grandfather there and my grandmother's reaction to him and just wanted to know what the big secret was.

You might not have noticed that I recently kept asking you about your grandfather. But your answer has always been the same. He was in the camp and moved to America after the war. And you always claimed you didn't know anything more. Today I know more, and I can't imagine that you didn't at some point find this out for yourself. But I don't want to spare you from knowing how I found out.

In the next few days I kept thinking about how I could at least start a conversation with my grandmother with some innocuous question that could then lead to the right answer later. But whenever I saw grandmother, I didn't dare. Onju sat stone-faced in her armchair all day, looking straight ahead and often didn't seem to know where she was. But the worst part was that she no longer wanted to go to the temple.

I tried my luck with my parents. It didn't work. They wouldn't tell me anything, either.

One night when everyone was already in bed, I got up and got myself a glass of water. I saw my mother come out of her bedroom. She went into the living room and turned on the television. She does that often when she can't sleep. I sat down with her and simply asked her what was going on with grandmother and told her what had happened at temple, but all she said was that there were things in life one could not talk about. She asked me not to torture anyone with my curiosity, and certainly not grandmother.

At the end of that week, on Sunday morning, the doorbell rang. I was still in bed, my father was making breakfast as he does every Sunday and went to the door. My room is right next to the front door. I heard my father speaking with a man, it sounded like an argument, which grew louder and more intense. I slipped out of bed, put on my robe and opened my bedroom door a little.

My father had the front door open a crack, but blocked the entrance with his foot, so the other man could not enter. I didn't know who was at the door, but the voice sounded familiar.

Go away – This is senseless – my father said.

But the other answered, he had to come in, that he couldn't live like this anymore, he would explain everything, and then he would also be understood. But my father raised his voice more and more and told him to leave.

Then I recognized the voice. It was your grandfather who was at the door. I didn't care if anyone saw me. I opened the door a little more and sat on the floor, with my ears at the opening so I could hear every word.

Your grandfather talked for a long, long time. His story didn't seem to have an end. He talked about his youth. He only wanted to survive just like everybody else in those difficult times. Nobody, he assured my father, died by his hand. On the contrary, he had been able to help hundreds, hid them, got food for them. He began to cry, begged to be allowed to see my grandmother once more, hammered on the door and pushed himself against it to force his way into the apartment.

Then I heard the shuffling steps of my grandmother. He couldn't see her, wailed, begged, threw himself against the door that my father kept closed with all his strength.

Go away! Onju said to my father, while she was standing behind him.

I could no longer restrain myself and pulled the door back far enough to see into the corridor. My father had stepped aside and Onju had opened the door. Your grandfather was on his knees. He looked up at my grandmother. His face was contorted, his eyes red, and I thought to myself, that's how a dying person looks.

She looked at him for a while and then said in a quiet, slightly trembling voice: If you really want me to, I forgive you. I forgive you that you picked my husband out of the line, because he refused to give your friend the bed in the corner. I forgive you, you miserable bastard, that I've had to live half my life alone because of this absurdity, and that you, like many others of his so-called friends, that all of you ...

Suddenly she trembled, seemed to be falling. My father, who was standing behind her, grabbed her under the arms and slowly put her on the floor. It was a strange picture, my grandmother sitting on the floor and your grandfather kneeling before her.

At that moment, my father kicked the door and it shut with a loud bang. Get out of here! he yelled. Or I'll call the police. He tried to lift Onju, but she was stiff as a board and her legs were spread out. So he sat down beside her and put his arms around her shoulder. Outside it was quiet.

Onju didn't cry. She had an almost peaceful face, nodded a few times, suddenly looked around and saw me sitting in the doorway of my room on my knees. For only a brief moment, we locked eyes. But it seemed to me like she was saying: Do you understand me now? Then she shook my father's arm off her shoulder. What's wrong with you? she said loudly. Are you going let me sit here on the floor forever? Am I going to eat breakfast here?

It was comforting to hear these discontented, sullen tones again. My father jumped up and helped her to her feet. I got up, too.

And then it was a beautiful Sunday. Onju was in the best mood she had been in for ages. She complained about everything, made jokes about my mother's cooking skills and threatened to move into a nursing home if she did not finally learn how to make grilled fish right. My father, she explained, had always been too stupid to succeed in business, and that she had warned her daughter before they got married.

But she didn't speak to me. Only in the evening when I was going to bed and started to give her a good-night kiss, she said very softly, so only I could hear her, I know that you like Robert. Don't blame him. It's not his fault. He is a very nice boy. It was only his grandfather, he has nothing to do with it.

But Onju, I said, how shall I ...

She put her finger to my lips. Be quiet. It would be

the worst thing for me if this affects your life, too. So, now go to sleep.

I kissed her on the cheek and went to my room.

This is, Robert, what I wanted to tell you. Do you know now what I know? Can you imagine what happened back then with our grandparents?

And you, Robert? Who are you? The grandson of a kapo? The son of the son of a kapo? Or just my boyfriend Robert? How can I forget what I have seen at home when I see you? How can I just go for a walk with you, sit beside you at the movies somewhere in the back row, where it is dark and no one can see us? Laugh with you or listen to your stories from a faraway world? Robert, I'm desperate, what should I do?

Your Sonja

Slansky was only able to read the last page of the letter haltingly. Tears ran down his face, dripped onto the paper, he kept wiping them away and continued reading. He no longer looked left or right, didn't care about the rabbi, was instead only absorbed by these words of a seventeen-year-old girl that were so terrible to him.

When he had read the last sentence, he carefully re-folded the damp letter and looked for a handkerchief to wipe his face. He took off his glasses and wiped them until the lenses were dry. Then he put them back on, turned to his side and asked the rabbi, "Now what ..."

But the narrow corridor to the stairs and the elevator, where the rabbi had been leaning against the wall and listening, was empty. No one stood there. ■

The Memory

HIS PARENTS named him Christoph. Three weeks before the due date calculated by the doctor, Thomas, Christoph's father, a small, roundish pharmaceutical representative, came home carrying a book that explained the meanings of surnames. Josefine, the mother of Christoph, liked the name. The origin was clear, as was its provenance; it was an everyday name and also easy to write.

Josefine – the daughter of a police officer – towered over Thomas by a head, was considerably heavier and somewhat younger. She worked as a teacher and taught six to ten year olds, loved to read American detective stories best of all, and liked to eat dark chocolate. Her mother had left her father soon after her birth for a rich butcher who lived on the same street, and who opened a smaller business in a different part of town with the money he got from the hurried sale of his old shop.

Josefine grew up with her father, who often took her to the police station, where she played with old dolls beside his desk, and later, when she came to him after school, could listen to the various interrogations. In the small town, that didn't bother anyone.

She got to know Thomas after he visited one of the doctors in the town to show his products. That was the day the doctor was assaulted by a crazed patient, an old drunkard who didn't want to accept that the doctor couldn't give him medicine that would help him drink more but not get drunk. Thomas was sitting with the doctor and praised the advantages of a new anti-rheumatic agent when the desperate man tore into the examination room and aimed an old pistol at the doctor and at Thomas, too.

Josefine's father took all three to the police station, and Thomas had to make a witness statement and sign it. Since this lasted until the early afternoon, the moment came when Josefine, by now a certified teacher in the town, brought her father his lunch. He always ate a little late, not wanting to forgo the home cooked meal his daughter prepared. Josefine brought a sealed metal container that was divided into three parts. A soup was in one of them, in another was the meat with juice, and the cooked potatoes were in the third part.

She saw Thomas then, who, with a nervous sweaty face, sat on a shabby wooden chair, a sample bag on his knees. He kept insisting he was only in the examination room of the doctor by chance and had nothing to do with the matter. Here his voice cracked, made him appear more ridiculous than anxious. Josefine looked at him and laughed. When he saw her happy face, his whole situation seemed more cheerful, and at least he stopped trembling.

He visited her over the next few months during his

repeated travels from one doctor to another, and invited her to dinner when he spent the night in her town. He stayed in the old inn "Zur Post" and always took the same room. It was the only one with a shower and a private bathroom. Above the double bed, which actually consisted of two single beds hewn from dark wood that were pushed together, hung a picture of a saint who carried a small child in his arm. When Thomas came, the owner had to take down this picture before his arrival. This was the only condition Thomas made.

One evening, when Thomas was back in town sitting with Josefine at the inn, she managed to seduce him. He always drank a little vodka along with some water before eating but otherwise no alcohol. When the waiter, as usual, poured a little out of the bottle into the small glass, Josefine asked him to leave the bottle on the table and to bring her a shot glass. She filled hers to the brim, downed it with a flourish, a few drops ran down her lips. She stuck out her tongue far enough to reach the corners of her mouth and looked Thomas in the eye as she licked off what remained.

Again and again, she ran her tongue slowly in circles over her upper and lower lips, and the light above the table was reflected in the moisture. Thomas also emptied his glass in one gulp, and Josefine filled it immediately, looking deeply into his eyes, and spilled some vodka on the table, which immediately seeped into the old wood. Both refilled their shot glasses with vodka, like beer tankards, and hurled the clear liquid into their bodies until Josefine suddenly stood up and took his hand.

"Come on, let's go!"

"But why, where?"

"Come on, let's go upstairs."

"We haven't eaten yet."

"We'll eat afterwards."

She squeezed her plump body out between the chair and table without letting go of his hand, took the room key lying between the glasses, and pulled Thomas behind her to where his room was on the first floor. Inside, she slowly unbuttoned her blouse, and Thomas remembered the many scenes in the examination rooms of doctors, where he waited to praise his medications, while a patient took off or put on her clothes. And when Josefine hiked her skirt over her hips, he thought of the next day, the next doctor, the next meeting, the next invoice, the next night in the next town.

"What's wrong with you? Don't you want to take off your clothes?" She stood there in her slip, had already taken off everything under it, and through the thin white fabric a solid, pink body shimmered and jiggled with every word.

She turned off the light, walked up to him in the dark, took his head in both hands and kissed him, and as she slipped the jacket off his shoulders and he tried to bend down to pick it up off the floor, she held him back.

"Leave it!"

Then she undressed him like he was a little boy, and he felt how he got smaller and smaller, surrounded by the smell of a freshly opened bottle of milk, and just let everything happen. He lay burrowed on his back in a sagging mattress, and a mountain moved over him silently until it plopped down on the bed next to him, exhausted and panting.

Thomas looked at the ceiling and noticed for the first time that many tiny dots were glued on to it that shone like little stars in the darkness. He tried to remember times long ago in another life that had come to an end. He wanted to venture into this era and pierce this heaven, but it held tight, a sky of concrete and steel. It was too far away, this past, and that was a good thing.

A little later they sat again in the dining room and ate soup, boiled beef and potatoes. Thomas stroked the sleeve of his jacket again and again and tried to clean off the white fibers that had gotten stuck everywhere. Josefine smiled at him, and he smiled back at her. His sales route had always taken a week, and he never had to spend more than a day in any city. It started in the same place every Monday and ended on Friday in his hometown. Some doctors also had small pharmacies and ordered directly from Thomas. Others only wrote prescriptions, and he tried to convince them that his company's products were better than the competition. He had a colorful brochure for each drug, which he opened as he made his presentation. Words and images fit together and made a convincing argument.

"Why are you doing this line of work? You understand so much about medicine, why are you a traveling salesman?" a lung specialist once asked him as they were discussing shadows on the lungs of a tuberculosis patient in an X-ray.

"I wanted to be a doctor but something came up, and I couldn't finish my studies."

When Thomas drove back to the city a week later, he

was anxious about this trip for the first time because Josefine was waiting for him. He even wanted to change his route, something he had never done before.

The phone rang as he reluctantly sorted out his sample bag.

"Hello Thomas! Is it you? Are you coming back today?"

"Where did you get my phone number?"

"Your office. I said I was the assistant of Doctor so-and-so and needed to talk to you. Good, wasn't it?"

He met her again that evening, and they repeated the evening just as it was the week before, and for the next three months.

For Thomas the weekly meetings with Josefine became an integral part of his tour. The time, the place, the event, the farewell – one of the many recurrences in his uniform life.

After about four months, something unexpected happened. Josefine waited on a wooden bench in the dining room at the agreed time. She was not alone. Her father, who towered over even her, sat next to her with a gloomy face and sucked again and again on his pipe, whose mouthpiece was completely chewed up.

Thomas looked at them feeling somewhat awkward. He didn't have a pleasant memory of his last meeting with Josefine's father in the town detention center, and people in uniform frightened him.

For a few seconds Thomas stood in front of them in his long coat and with his packed sample bag, and no one moved. Then Josefine's father suddenly jumped up, rushed to Thomas, embraced him and kissed him on both cheeks. His rough beard left red spots on Thomas's delicate face.

He dropped the bag in shock; it fell over, opened and some colorful boxes of medication tumbled out. Thomas wanted to bend over in order to pick up the items and put them back into the bag, but Josefine had already rushed from the table and was collecting the boxes; closing the bag she handed it to him with a smile, so that Thomas immediately suspected what this meeting was all about.

They moved him to the bench, pulled his coat from his shoulders, and her father ordered a bottle of champagne and three glasses from the innkeeper, who was watching the goings on with a grin on his face. As though he had been waiting for this command, in a few short moments he had the bottle and glasses on a tray and served them with exaggerated movements, opened the bottle with a loud bang, filled the three glasses, and waited for the solemn announcement with the bottle in hand until her father gestured for him to move away.

At that moment Thomas knew Josefine was pregnant and that he should marry her. He pushed the glass back, it tipped over; he wanted to get off the narrow bench, slid to the edge of the table, but her father was standing there, put his hands on his shoulders and pushed him back. It was hopeless.

So they drank the cheap champagne, disgustingly sweet, and agreed on a date that was not that far from that evening. Thomas spoke repeatedly of difficulties and formalities that should be taken care of first, until her father angrily asked him if he was already married and was going to leave his daughter behind in disgrace.

"No, it's all right. I'm not married. I just don't have any papers."

"What kind of papers?" The father was restless and spoke loudly.

"You need all the documents about your parents to get married. And these have all been lost during the war." Thomas spoke quietly and didn't look at them.

Her father promised to take care of everything. After all, he was the town policeman.

It was a simple wedding, not a church wedding, no large wedding party. Only a few of Josefine's relatives attended. Nobody came from Thomas's family or friends. No one else was still alive, he said, or they had emigrated long ago to Australia. Despite her pregnancy, Josefine got drunk and threw up in the dining room during the banquet. Together with her father Thomas carried her up to his room. On the wedding night, he lay next to her crying in a black suit that was too tight for him.

After the wedding, they moved to the city where Thomas lived. From the beginning, Josefine was a concerned, caring woman. Movements and activities that had previously made up his life as a bachelor disappeared. She was like a shadow that he constantly saw next to him, moving in parallel, always there but not disturbing anything. When their son was born, the problems with the papers resurfaced. There were no documents about Thomas, except for his identity card. No birth certificate, no baptismal certificate, no marriage certificate of the parents. Josefine asked him again and again. She was eager to learn more about his family. He always gave her the same answer: "They all died in the war, and their documents were lost."

Thomas remained a man without a past, without memories, without old photographs and without stories from earlier years. He got nervous when Josefine asked him about his parents, contradicted himself, described his mother once as blond and tall, then again as small and dark. He apologized, stuttering that his memories about them were confused by the early loss of his parents. Josefine, who very soon felt this topic was unpleasant to him and changed his usually calm and controlled way into its opposite, decided to stop asking him about this. She loved him as he was, and present and future were more important to her than stories from a time they hadn't spent together in the first place.

The past remained a deep lake, where everything disappeared and never resurfaced, and if you stared at it with intense concentration, there was nothing to be seen but the dark blue sky, which was reflected in the calm water.

Christoph, their son, grew up to be a magnificent specimen. His bright hair darkened a little over the years, his mouth was maybe a little too big, his lips too drawn apart, causing the face to look almost feminine, in contrast to his strong, athletic body. He attended the public school near their apartment. His teacher, a small, elderly woman nearing retirement, loved Christoph like the son she never had. He was allowed to sit in the front row and was responsible for the chalk and the blackboard eraser, took four of these white, dusty chalk sticks from the office every morning and placed them according to size parallel to each other on the teacher's small table, dipped a sponge in fresh water and cleaned the blackboard until it was clean and dry when class began.

Some years later they moved into a terraced row house. Christoph was now ten years old, and Thomas had been promoted to regional manager. He controlled a large area, supervised six employees and only had to visit the important and difficult clients. He spent his evenings at home and could watch his son grow up, how his body became more angular and tough, and the lines around his well-trained muscles deepened.

Christoph was an excellent athlete. Every year he got new ski and tennis equipment, and in summer and winter, vacation spots were selected as to provide the necessary environment for practice. By sixteen Christoph had broad shoulders, was a head taller than his father, and a dozen trophy cups were in his bedroom, tokens of both small and large triumphs.

But with the freedoms of youth came the fears of old age. Thomas loved his only son so deeply and fanatically that more and more often he jerked awake from a short, light sleep in his well-worn favorite chair, drenched in sweat and trembling, because the idea or dream tormented him that his son might have an accident one day. Thomas began to have panic attacks, tried to hold his now almost seventeen-year-old son's hand when they crossed a street, and couldn't go to bed when Christoph was out with friends in the evening.

Every separation, even leaving the house every day to go to school, could mean the permanent loss of his son. Thomas hugged Christoph, kissed him on the lips, and clenched his teeth to keep tears from welling up. A few weeks later, he tried to arrange his lunch break so he could pick Christoph up from school, drive him home and hurry back to his office.

Josefine, who in the beginning was moved by Thomas's

sudden concerns – he had been friendly but distant to his son up until now – was afraid he was well on his way to going crazy. She urged him, first cautiously, then firmly, to see a doctor. And Thomas had no objections to her proposal because he felt his changed behavior was making him a nervous wreck.

Once during dinner, when their son had again gone out with friends and Thomas kept looking at the clock and nervously asked when Christoph intended to come home and who these friends were with whom he was spending his time with, Josefine said, "Maybe the reason for your panic lies hidden in an experience you have not processed, with your mother perhaps, or with your siblings. I don't know much about you, you never talk about it, who knows what happened when you were a boy that makes you suffer so much worrying about what might happen to your son."

The result was a catastrophe. Thomas, a soup spoon in his hand, stared at her, began to tremble, his face alternately pale and beet red, put the spoon next to the plate and shouted: "No. It was nothing, nothing! I've forgotten everything, it is like it's erased, like a document that was written in pencil."

"But there must be documents, Thomas, in the archives, in the registry offices, proof of birth, a note about the parents, it's not possible for everything to disappear everywhere."

He suddenly stood up, his chair tipped back, he slammed his fist on the table, rattling the glasses, and yelled: "No. damn it, there's nothing, nothing! Do you understand me, no archives – no documents – leave my family in peace. Let it go! Leave me in peace, finally –"

He had never reacted so violently, and Josefine was so surprised that she almost had to laugh at the by now round, balding little Thomas and his outburst. She decided not to talk about this matter ever again.

Christoph didn't have an easy time at school but got his high school diploma with the help of a number of tutors. He decided to major in physical education.

Thomas reached the retirement age, spent the whole day at home and worried even more about Christoph. As a completely unathletic man, it was inconceivable to him that a young man would voluntarily hang high above a floor from wooden rings fastened to ropes and swing back and forth, or do gymnastics on steel bars, hike in the mountains through deep snow in winter, jump into a swimming pool from a tower and be able to perform contortions on the way down.

He began to follow Christoph secretly and watch him. Hidden behind a tree, he saw the students as they ran through the forest, or slipped into a chair in the empty sports stadium where they trained. He spent entire days watching Christoph, and his stomach cramped every time the activities of his son seemed too dangerous.

The empty days of doing nothing passed, and Josefine, who had been aware of her husband's secret investigations for a long time, didn't mind since at least in this way he was out in the fresh air.

One day, something strange happened. Thomas waited, as he did every Tuesday afternoon – he had committed Christoph's schedule to memory long ago – at the football field for the students who practiced there, but was shocked when he saw his son. Christoph was not alone.

Holding hands, he came with a dark-haired girl, and when they sat down on a bench, he kissed her before he pulled off the sweat pants he was wearing over his gym shorts and ran to the the others in the center of the field.

That evening, Thomas felt compelled to ask his son who the girl was. But he could not talk to anyone about it because he still thought no one knew he was constantly following Christoph. He paced restlessly in the living room, sat down in his chair, and constantly changed the TV channel until Josefine finally asked him what was wrong.

"Does our Christoph have a girlfriend?" he asked Josefine.

"Yes. Didn't you know?"

"Who is she? What's her name? Why doesn't he bring her home?"

"Her name is Miriam, he hasn't known her for long, we ..."

"What's her name?"

"Miriam!"

Thomas jumped up when he heard the name. "How did she get this name? It's unusual!"

Josefine didn't see anything unusual about the name and promised to invite the girl soon.

A week later, Miriam came for dinner. She was small and thin, and her bright eyes were in strange contrast to the dark hair that framed her head with large curls. She had dressed up for dinner with Christoph's parents, wearing a white blouse, tight gray trousers and a jacket that otherwise only men wore.

Josefine sat with them in the living room. All three had

a glass of sherry in front of them, and they all waited for Thomas. Half an hour before Christoph and Miriam were expected, Thomas had suddenly declared he had to go to the main post office, which was open evenings. At issue was a letter he could not send the next morning since it would be too late by then. He didn't hear Josefine asking what was so important about the letter, because he was already out the door.

It got later and later, and they began to eat without him. They silently ate the thick soup with finely chopped vegetables; only the soft sounds of a spoon clattering against a plate could be heared. Josefine became anxious before she brought the roast to the table. What had happened to Thomas? Christoph calmed her and tried to distract everyone by talking about the future. Miriam would soon be finished with her studies and would surely get a job as a translator, so then they could afford an apartment together. He would look for a position as a gym coach for the next school year, and if he found one everything would work out.

He looked at Miriam with a smile and took her hand, a gesture that reminded Josefine of times long past. But she only considered these timeless declarations of love for a moment before she returned her thoughts to Thomas, his strange behavior towards this woman, his desperate defense of his past and his escape.

Thomas came home drunk for the first time since he married Josefine. Christoph found his father asleep sitting by the door when he came back after taking Miriam home. Thomas sat on the top stone step at the entrance of the terraced row house with his back against the door, snoring loudly and regularly. Along with Christoph, Josefine dragged him up the narrow, winding stairs to the first floor and slowly laid him out on the carpet. Thomas lay on his back like a package tied with string and didn't move. They peeled him out of his coat and pulled off his shoes, pants and jacket. Then he woke up confused and asked where he was, tried to get up, staggered and fell to his knees, pulled himself up by the end of the double bed and walked straight into the bathroom.

When they asked him whether he needed help, he yelled back that they should leave him alone. Everything was all right. They waited outside the bathroom, and Thomas came out composed and sober, put on his pajamas without saying a word and got into bed.

The next morning, he refused to talk about what had happened the evening before. He said over and over again that he could not remember anything, and it didn't make any sense to ask him about it.

But everything was just put on hold, postponed until the moment of truth. In the coming months, Miriam came back to visit several times, but Thomas managed to see her only very briefly or not at all every time she visited. He refused any discussion about it with Josefine, and when Christoph once asked whether he had a problem with Miriam, he denied this ardently and assured him that in his opinion she was a really fine woman.

Half a year later Christoph, Josefine and Thomas were invited over by Miriam's parents. And this time Josefine prevented any attempt by Thomas to avoid the meeting. The entire afternoon she did not let him out of her sight and as the evening approached, Thomas was very quiet, put on his best suit, Josefine straightened his tie and then the three of them left the house.

When they stood in front of the house where Miriam lived, Josefine begged Thomas to behave himself that evening, no matter what happened.

"What do you mean?"

She didn't answer him, opened the door, and they climbed slowly up the stairs to the third floor. Miriam's parents lived in a large apartment, in a building that was constructed about a hundred years ago. The rooms had high ceilings, the furniture came from another time, and the carpets and paintings nearly turned these rooms where they lived their everyday lives into a museum.

They knocked on the front door with its gold-plated nameplate. The father of Miriam, who opened the door for them, had a round, dark blue, flat cap on his head, embroidered with a few letters in silver thread.

He greeted them loudly and heartily, helped Josefine out of her coat and led the guests into the dining room, where a long, festive table stood. Waiting for them were Miriam, her mother and an elderly couple who were introduced as her father's parents.

Thomas' hand was so moist he repeatedly wiped it on the side of his pants before he offered it to anyone. Without returning a greeting, he looked at the strange people, wide-eyed and mute, as they shook his hand. Josefine tried to pull Thomas to the side, after they had all greeted each other, and whispered, "I didn't dare tell you, but Miriam's parents are Jews."

The blood had drained from Thomas's face. He just nodded and tried to keep the yarmulke that Miriam's father had put on him from slipping off his bald head.

Miriam's father walked up and asked them to come to the table. He took Thomas by the arm and led him to a chair that stood on the narrow side of the table. As they walked through the room, he quietly told him they were not very religious, neither ate kosher nor kept the Shabbat, but on Friday nights the family would meet and eat together.

Thomas didn't answer him, trembled all over, let himself plop into the chair, and wiped his sweaty forehead with a napkin.

"Are you feeling well?" Miriam's mother asked.

Thomas didn't respond to the question.

"He's just a little tired," Josefine said with a desperate smile.

Miriam's father went to the other end of the table. Next to Thomas sat Miriam's mother, a beautiful, proud woman with dark hair like her daughter. She wore a dark blue, simple dress, but her hands were adorned with jewelry, and several different long chains were garlanded around her neck. Josefine sat next to Thomas on the other side, watching him nervously and was ready to prevent the worst, whatever that might be.

Suddenly they all got up, and Miriam's father filled the silver, engraved Kiddush cup to the brim with red wine. But when he took the cup and lifted it gently, Thomas walked, hesitantly at first, but then with two, three quick steps around the table.

They all stared at him and Josefine exclaimed: "Thomas, what is it?" She tried to follow him and stop him.

He pushed her away with a deliberate motion and took

the cup with trembling hands. Slowly, he raised it without spilling a drop and held it in front of himself over the table, and spoke in a singing tone: "*Barukh ata Adonai Eloheinu, Melekh ha'olam, bo're p'ri hagafen*...." Then he drank the whole cup, put it on the table and went back to his place with a smile on his face.

No one in the room moved. It was so quiet everyone tried to breathe as quietly as possible, because even that sound was disturbing.

Thomas saw Josefine's eyes, and his eyes slowly welled up with tears. "I lied to you. Forgive me." He spoke softly and unevenly, and the words came so slowly that they almost lost their meaning.

And, at once, Josefine understood everything, went up to this little man she had always loved, took his head in her hands, and kissed him. ■

The Coffin Birth

I T WAS Mr. Bernstein's seventieth birthday. Guests came from far away, and the celebration had been prepared for weeks.

Mr. Bernstein's house was in the middle of town in a previously exclusive residential area where only a few old buildings remained standing. What the bombs had not destroyed was later demolished, dismantled and leveled for new construction. But his house still stood. As it did a hundred years ago, when it was built by a textile manufacturer among the villas that belonged to other industrialists. Mr. Bernstein was rich, very rich even. He had the right to live in such a house, and he was proud of it.

His seventieth birthday was also the fiftieth anniversary of his survival. Yes, he was in fact a survivor, and over the past fifty years that he had lived in freedom, he tried to prove to the world that he had not survived in vain. Now he sat on a radiator in his study, which was on the first floor of the villa, and looked out the window at the garden. The lawn was beautifully cared for, the roses stood in groups arranged by color.

What a long way he had come from his small Polish town, from the small one-story house made of rough bricks, with water in the courtyard and sawdust strewn every Friday on the wooden floor and swept. But to whom could he show this wealth? His father was dead, murdered in the camp, dragged away in front of his eyes. His mother died before the German invasion. His siblings disappeared, his aunts and uncles, who knows where the ashes of their scorched bodies were buried. No one had survived, except him.

He heard the voices and the steps of the visitors who walked up and down in the reception rooms on the second floor above as they waited for the beginning of the festivities. Was the Chancellor there perhaps already? And the mayor? The leaders of the opposition party? The representatives of the big banks, the chemical companies and the auto industry? Are there twenty? Or thirty? Or even a hundred?

The door opened and Mrs. Bernstein entered. She, too, had survived. In another camp. She, too, had been alone after the war, and when they met each other in an infirmary, they thought their shared fate was enough to bind them together, and they got married.

"Why don't you come up? Everyone is waiting for you!"

Mr. Bernstein shrugged.

"What's wrong?" She said it quietly, and it didn't sound like a question.

"What about my birthday present?"

"I don't know, I think ..." Both were silent for a moment.

"But it was decided that she would announce it today," he said with an almost lachrymose voice.

She didn't hear this tone very often from him. Mr.

Bernstein was accustomed to saying what he wanted with a harsher tone. Hardly anyone around him, not even his wife and daughter, dared to talk back to him. He had built an empire from nothing. During the first years after the war, he had developed his business with incredible skill and had used the short-term paralysis of the competitors to his advantage. When he became rich, the tributes came all by themselves. The ostracized thanked him that he had forgiven them their crimes.

Mrs. Bernstein, who had been a faithful wife to him all these years, went a couple of steps toward him and held out her hand.

He moved away. "Is she here?" he asked again.

"Maybe, yes, I think so –"

"And?"

"Apparently, Lisa has not yet decided."

"She's thirty-three – How long do we have to wait? I only have one daughter –"

Now Mrs. Bernstein shrugged.

"Where is my family? Where are my grandchildren? Where is my son-in-law? And who do I pass my business on to? What was the point of all this? Then I could have gone the same way my father went –" He staggered slightly, steadied himself on the desk. "Get her down here – I want to talk to her!"

"Lisa?"

"No. The *schatchen* – I've paid this matchmaker for three years! What for?"

"If you insist – I'll go see if she's here."

Mrs. Bernstein left the room quietly and carefully, walked up to the second floor and searched among the guests for Yasmine. She found her at the bar holding a glass of orange juice.

"Excuse me, please, Yasmine, may I speak with you for a moment?"

"Oh, Mrs. Bernstein, what a wonderful party –" said the lady who was chatting with Yasmine. She talked too loudly, her jewelry was too heavy, and the opening of her dress was too revealing for her age and body.

Mrs. Bernstein tugged on Yasmine's arm. "My husband wants to see you. He's waiting for a decision –"

"I'm not ready yet, I can't just promise something –"

"Oh God, what shall I do now? Everything is so hard for him – He'll kill himself – Come with me, you have to help me now!"

They both went down into the study. In the stairwell Mrs. Bernstein held Yasmine back by the arm. "You promised – Otherwise there will be a disaster this evening!"

"Never mind, I'll think of something –"

"I hope – I hope for your sake –"

"What does that mean?" Yasmine looked at her sharply.

"You know what I mean –"

"Don't threaten me. If you tell him, it will only harm you –"

Mrs. Bernstein didn't answer her.

Mr. Bernstein received them in a bad mood and tore into Yasmine, "What's going on? We had a deal – For today!"

"I can't help you, Mr. Bernstein. I've tried everything in recent weeks. I got a professor for Lisa, a bank manager, I even tried it with an artist – Nothing worked – One person might still work who Lisa has known for some time. They will consider it, the two of them ... so she says."

"And? What is the problem? There must be a reason. She isn't twenty anymore –"

"I don't know. They meet once, twice, sometimes three times, then it's off again."

"Maybe you selected the wrong guys, my daughter is very picky. Surely it can't be so difficult, that's ridiculous. I'm now seventy – How long should I wait? I have no descendants, no grandchildren –"

"Calm down." Mrs. Bernstein tried to approach him again, but he backed away.

There was a knock at the door.

"What is it?"

David came in, Mr. Bernstein's assistant. "Excuse me, Mr. Bernstein. They are all here. They are waiting for you –"

Mr. Bernstein nodded and sent him back to the guests.

David was a slender young man who had grown up and studied in the United States. Later he returned to the country his father had once fled.

Yasmine caught up with David in the stairwell and took him by the arm. "You must help me –" she whispered and as she talked to him, she got more and more loud and intense.

David pushed her back, shook his head and wriggled from her grasp. "I won't do it. That's ridiculous!"

"Please, I beg you –" She pleaded with him and clasped her hands as though in prayer. "You'll be killing him, if you don't help me –"

David just left her standing there. Yasmine followed him and didn't stop gesturing, pushed him from behind with her hand until he sped up and ran upstairs.

Mr. and Mrs. Bernstein slowly climbed up the stairs to the second floor. Mr. Bernstein held on to a gold-plated rod that hung on a wall from thick ropes. He pulled himself up, step by step, and it could be seen on his face how resistant he was. Among all the paintings and expensive furniture in the large hall on the second floor the waiting guests stood, holding their glasses. A loud "Ah" echoed through the hall as the honoree appeared. They put their glasses aside and began to applaud. "Bravo!" cried some, "Live long!" cried others.

One of the guests in a dark blue double-breasted suit, which was obviously too small for his bulk, tapped a spoon against his glass. It became quiet, but he began to speak even before it was completely silent.

"The Chancellor, where is the Chancellor?" whispered some, and others hissed for silence.

The speaker began with a joke, continued with a serious analysis of the past and finally reached the present, which he posed as the high point in the life of Mr. Bernstein. He added praise and acknowledgment, counted deeds and events, and mentioned again and again his personal experience with the honoree.

It was a fine speech, and some wiped tears from their eyes. Mr. Bernstein, concluded the speaker, is the living symbol of reconciliation. Then he went to Mr. Bernstein and hugged him, and the applause reached its high point.

Guests lined up one behind the other to congratulate the guest of honor. He thanked everyone, and nobody realized how unhappy he was.

Lisa came too late. She had missed the speech, but now she was here, went to her father and took him by the shoulders. "All the best, Papa!"

She kissed him on both cheeks. He tried to turn his head to touch her lips, but she was faster. It had become a ritual between the two that repeated itself in such instances.

"Where is my son-in-law?" he whispered in her ear as she kissed him.

"All the best, Papa. I'm so happy for you. So many important people."

"Where is my birthday gift?" He stared into her eyes.

"All the best. I love you!" Then she turned around and let the next guest approach.

While Mr. and Mrs. Bernstein continued to receive congratulations, Lisa, Yasmine and David stood in a corner of the room.

"He won't believe it," David said, looking down, embarrassed.

Lisa put her hand on his. "That doesn't matter. The others will believe it, and that's enough –"

Lisa took David's hand and made her way through the crowd, impatiently pushing aside guests who were in the way until she reached her father.

"Quiet please!" she shouted at the crowd and smiled at her father. "We haven't given our gift to the birthday boy yet!"

Mrs. Bernstein reached the small group around Mr. Bernstein. She whispered something in Lisa's ear, but she went on without allowing herself to be interrupted.

"Today, I want to introduce to you my future fiancé: David, whom you all already know. He has, for many years, supported my father like no other. Without him, there would never have been this success. David and I have become closer over the years. In a few weeks we will be engaged." She turned to her father. "That, my dear Papa, is my birthday present!" She hugged and kissed him.

He held her firmly with both arms and looked in her eyes. "Is this really what you want?"

She just nodded, moved over to her mother and gave her a kiss. Mrs. Bernstein began to cry. Mr. Bernstein took David's hand and held it with both hands. He whispered something in his ear. David smiled as if in great pain and shook his head fiercely.

The guests applauded and shouted "Hurrah!" and "Bravo!"

David was passed around and kissed. They took his hand and squeezed it tightly. The men patted him on the shoulders, and more than a few muttered what a good choice he had made.

The black-clad waiters filled the glasses with champagne. The guests cheered the couple, Lisa kissed David the way she always kissed her father. David was passive and showed no emotion.

Mr. and Mrs. Bernstein stood somewhat apart.

"Why didn't I notice anything?" Mr. Bernstein asked his wife.

"I didn't know about it, either –"

"How long has this been going on?"

"I don't know."

"I just hope that she will be happy." Mr. Bernstein wiped the sweat from his forehead.

"Of course." Mrs. Bernstein's eyes became smaller and smaller. She searched for her husband's hand, and they both stood as motionless as two statues.

"Do you think she loves him?" Mr. Bernstein asked his wife.

"The way I loved you when we got married."

"That's not an answer –"

"But it's the truth!"

They were still standing there, not moving, while Lisa and David, surrounded by their friends, were pulled away.

The party had no further significance for Mr. Bernstein. Apathetic, he let everything wash over him, courteously answered the questions that were put to him, and thanked his guests for extending their congratulations.

Several hours later, he sat alone in his office in front of a box of old photos. The last guests had left long ago, and Mrs. Bernstein had retired for the evening. He rummaged in the box filled with images from the past. He didn't like old photos. All these people were dead and hardly any of them had a gravestone. Not even his own father was buried in a cemetery. All disappeared, kidnapped, annihilated. On the back of many photographs there was no mention of a name or a date. A little girl wearing a summer dress in a meadow. Who was she? Was she still alive? Old men with beards and black hats wearing clothes he could still remember well. Everything gone. Only I'm still here, but what comes after me? he thought.

As much as he admired David, his assistant, he also knew that this alleged forthcoming engagement had been staged only for him. David had everything he had always missed in himself, had to acquire with difficulty and had never really made his own. Even to witness David's fine table manners was embarrassing when he sat at the same table. David as a son-in-law? What a dream, if it were only true!

He lost himself in fantasies, visualized a Friday evening with his family, the grandchildren, the guests, the in-laws. Saturday morning David would stand beside him in the front row, and they would both be called for their blessing, and everyone would envy him. And in a few years, little David would sit between them with a tiny Kippot that would keep sliding down his curly head.

Maybe everything will still work out, Mr. Bernstein thought for a moment, and looked at the photo of a young couple. It was a wedding photo, but without names. He tore the photo up and threw it in the trash. What was the point of picking through all these photographs? Life was what counted! It's not death that counts, it's life! That was the saying that had kept him alive until he was freed by the Russians, half naked and emaciated.

Life, yes, life.

He had to go up to see his daughter. He wanted to encourage her, to avow how much he was pleased about the engagement to David.

Lisa had a small apartment in her parent's home. The top floor under the roof had been rebuilt with a small living room, a bedroom, a separate kitchen and a bathroom. She had a private entrance to the apartment, but one could also access it from the rooms below.

Mr. Bernstein took the elevator to the fourth floor. From here, a small, winding staircase led to Lisa's apartment. He climbed the stairs slowly, tired from the long day, but also happy about the possibility that the future promised him. He stopped in front of her door, breathless, and waited a moment. He didn't want to ring the bell. The bell didn't make a distinction between whether someone was waiting outside on the street or in front of the door. He had a key on his key chain and opened the door quietly. It was dark. She seemed to be asleep.

Mr. Bernstein was about to leave the apartment when he heard soft music. He was happy that she seemed to be still awake, and went to her bedroom. The door was ajar, a faint glimmer of light penetrated under the door gap. He pushed the door open slowly. Lisa had a beautiful bedroom, its walls painted flat red and a skylight in the center of the ceiling through which one saw the stars in the dark sky on a clear night. Under the window was a large round bed that Mr. Bernstein had given Lisa for her thirtieth birthday. She had always wanted a round bed. A bearskin rug lay in front of the bed. The walls were covered with black and white graphics that Lisa had collected over the years. The furniture had been built to fit elegantly into the slope under the roof, and the dark wood went well with the bearskin on the floor and the paint on the wall. He liked this room.

"Papa! What are you doing here?"

He had not yet seen the bed. Now he set his eyes on his daughter, who was sitting up in bed, naked, the covers pressed against her breasts. Beside her, Yasmine. In her shock, she had forgotten to cover herself, and sat cross-legged next to Lisa. She was also naked. Completely naked.

"Papa, I can explain this!" Lisa jumped out of bed and tried to wrap the cover around her body.

Mr. Bernstein backed away until he came up against the wall.

"Papa, everything is all right. Don't worry. Everything is the way you want it to be. Yasmine and I are getting married, and I'll let myself be artificially inseminated with David's semen. You'll get your grandchild, and I'll get Yasmine."

Mr. Bernstein could feel how weak his knees were.

"Isn't that right, Yasmine –" said Lisa, and Yasmine nodded silently.

Mr. Bernstein was afraid he was going to fall and braced his hands against the wall.

He looked at his daughter with weary eyes and then at Yasmine, who still, without stirring, sat naked on the bed. What a beautiful woman, he thought as he looked at Yasmine. The long brown hair, short bangs on the fore-head, the narrow face and large, dark blue eyes.

Yasmine tried to cover her breasts with both hands, but she succeeded only partially, and the picture that presented itself to Mr. Bernstein became even more erotic. She sat cross-legged, so Mr. Bernstein's gaze could not miss anything.

"Papa, are you listening to me?"

But Mr. Bernstein pushed his daughter aside and walked towards the bed. Yasmine sat rigid and motionless on the bed.

"How beautiful you are," Mr. Bernstein said, as he slowly shuffled in his slippers around the bed, sat down at the edge of it and stretched out his hand to her.

Yasmine did not move. She let his hand stroke her hair, neck, shoulder and breasts. Lisa stood motionless in the room without saying a word. When he kissed Yasmine's arm, Lisa took a step forward. "Papa! What...!"

"Shut up – Not another word!" Mr. Bernstein shouted. He threw her a look she knew. In such cases she had never dared to talk back to him.

Mr. Bernstein kissed Yasmine's neck, the nape of her neck, pressed the flat of his hand against her until she lay on her back, and with the other hand opened the cloth belt of his dressing-gown. He took Yasmine's hand and led it under the soft white robe.

"Shut your mouth. I don't want to hear one word!" he shouted to his daughter again, even though she hadn't said a word. She had retreated into a corner of the room and sat next to the wall, biting her fist.

Mr. Bernstein breathed heavily while Yasmine tried to fulfill his wishes. She had surrendered control of her movements, only functioned mechanically and found the entire situation so absurd that she didn't know whether to laugh or cry. Even as Mr. Bernstein let go of her arm, leaned back to brace himself and closed his eyes, she continued her work and clearly gave him great pleasure. Having this famous, rich and powerful man in her hands this way was fascinating. When Mr. Bernstein was on top of her and, thanks to her preparations, finished the business in a few short strokes, she had to laugh out loud.

Mr. Bernstein rolled to the side, lay for a moment on his back, breathing heavily. Then he stood up and walked over to his daughter. She perched as before, lifeless in a different part of the room, still wrapped in a blanket. While Mr. Bernstein fastened the belt of his dressing gown, he looked into her eyes, stood still for a few seconds and said, "So. Now you can marry her!"

Lisa lost her self-control and began to sob, loud and hard.

Mr. Bernstein left the room, took the elevator down to the floor where the bedrooms were, and slipped under the covers beside his wife. She lay awake in the dark and had waited for him.

"Where were you?" she asked him.

"Up with Lisa."

"So, what now?"

"Nothing, it's alright. Lisa is going to marry Yasmine. Then she will be inseminated, and we'll get a grandchild!"

Mrs. Bernstein turned to the side and switched on the light next to her bed. "What nonsense are you talking about?"

Mr. Bernstein sat up and smiled at his wife. "Such is life these days, what can we do?"

"That's terrible! I won't stand for it – And all this on your birthday –"

"It could be worse. I'm satisfied. I got my birthday present!"

Mr. Bernstein kissed his wife on the cheek, wished her a good night, rolled over and went to sleep happy and content. ■

Prague

I T WAS THE AUTUMN of 1968. I was sixteen when my
father told his editor that he could no longer work for
a newspaper that thought it fit to support the invasion
of Czechoslovakia by the Russians and their allies.

Three days later my mother received a letter. At the time,
she was working as the manager of a hotel that belonged
to the Peace Council, an organization that in turn was run
by the Russians. The building was in a lousy district of
Vienna near the Prater and was the only decent hotel in an
area where otherwise there were only brothels. The letter
was only a few words long and said she no longer needed
to come, but they would send her two month's salary.

So they were both suddenly unemployed in Vienna,
and I lost the theoretical basis for my worldview. Until
then, the world had been so easy. There was good, and
there was evil. The good – those were the countries that
were friends of the Soviet Union. Evil were all that were
dependent on the United States.

We lived in a small terraced house with a little garden

that was built shortly after the First World War. The walls were thin, the rooms small with low ceilings, and starting at seven-thirty at night you could hear the neighbor's TV. He was a policeman, with a wife who had a child when she was well over forty. He turned off the television depending on his shift, which alternated between day and night.

The district headquarters of the Communist Party was very close to our house. Through the backyard of a hardware store you could reach the two rooms, one of which was the office and the other the clubroom. A meeting of the youth organization was held here every Tuesday evening. At that time, I liked going there. First, there was a ping-pong table, and secondly, what was even more important was that girls my age and even older regularly came to the meetings. I loved watching them play table tennis, the way they started to sweat, how their white shirts became see-through, and how they opened one button after another to cool off.

One of the girls was named Katya. She was a year older than me and loved the theater. I think she wanted to be an actress. All week long, I flipped through the cultural pages of the newspaper my father worked for so I would be prepared for the next Tuesday evening.

One weekend, I read about a new play that got wonderful reviews. I didn't understand the text, but even I could tell that it was an important theater premiere. A group from France would be traveling to the festival in Vienna. The performance was being praised as "futuristic actionism," "groundbreaking" and "modernistic." The critic went on and on about it in this vein.

The next Tuesday evening, I asked Katya if she would

like to see the French play with me.

"Can you get tickets?" she beamed at me. She had a beautiful round face, and her brown, long hair reached far beyond her shoulders. When she laughed, she opened her eyes wide, and you had to do the same, it was just contagious. She also thrust her upper body forward, and her large breasts sprang at you. She usually wore long, colorful skirts that covered her rather large behind. I was hopelessly in love for the first time in my life, and I was sure I would marry her.

Only when she withdrew and read something, or didn't feel observed, did she purse her lips and become very sad. Sometimes I watched her without her noticing, and when her face suddenly changed and became serious, I wanted to go ask her what had happened, where her wonderful laughter had gone? I never did, but even the thought was beautiful.

"Yes, of course, that's not a problem for me," I replied. I had no idea that it might be difficult to get a couple of theater tickets.

At home, I asked my mother how I could get tickets to the French play.

She looked at me with her amused eyes and asked: "Since when do you like going to the theater?"

"Everyone starts sometime," I told her.

"But unfortunately, you're starting with the impossible. This play has been sold out for weeks. See something else. Just go to the Burgtheater, where the day after tomorrow they're playing 'Woe to Him Who Lies' by Grillparzer. This is a good one for you to start with."

I tried to explain to her that the French play was the

only play I absolutely needed to see. "Papa always gets press passes; he could give them to me."

"Unfortunately not anymore, that's over. Many things will be different now," she said with a sad voice and went into the kitchen, which ajoined the dining room.

The kitchen was tiny. Until a few years ago it had been part of the terrace that my parents later remodeled when my second brother was born and there were five of us in the family.

My mother didn't have work, my father didn't either; both were at home all day – it was not easy. My father was almost fifty years old and soon began to look for a new job. But who would hire a communist in Vienna, even if he were a former communist? Again and again he came home after a job interview teeming with optimism and told us how well it went. But a day or two later he received a letter, almost always using the same phrasing, that they were sorry, but they had decided otherwise.

My two brothers were four and ten years younger than me. The older one's name was Martin. He was small and skinny, wore thick glasses and was slated to one day become a university professor. Each Christmas – yes, we celebrated Christmas, not the Jewish holidays at home – so every Christmas, and also for his birthday, he got thick books about the histories of the Indians or the Greeks.

We didn't get along particularly well. My greatest fun when he was little was to tell jokes and fool around until he peed in his pants. He couldn't hold it back when he laughed. It was my small revenge on the genius of the family.

The younger of my two brothers was named Georg. My

mother was no longer very young when he was born, and she treated him as a gift for which one waits a long time and whose arrival one no longer believes.

But my worries were focused on the theater tickets for the French play. I decided to ask my father directly if he could help me. But then I remembered I had never asked him for anything. There was always this detour via my mother. My father was not very big, not very small; slender like my middle brother and also wore glasses. They looked very much alike.

For years I had only seen my father on weekends. He left in the morning for his newspaper office and came home late at night. On the weekends, we ate meals together and at least tried to talk about important things. On two sides of the large table in the dining room were two chairs, where my father and my mother sat. The corner bench reached around the other two sides of the table. Martin sat on the short side, my mother facing him. Georg had a seat next to me on the long side. He sat to my left, my father sat facing us.

This Sunday, when I had planned to ask my father for the theater tickets, we had Rindsrouladen. First, a vegetable soup, then the meat with rice and steamed carrots. My mother brought the soup bowl from the kitchen.

"The soup spoon is missing!" she said to my father in this severe tone she almost always used when she spoke to us. He jumped up and got it out of the silverware drawer. She hated it when something wasn't in its proper place.

I decided to ask him about the tickets while we were eating the soup. I was determined to talk about my troubles before another topic could come up for discussion.

"There's something important we want to tell you." My mother beat me to the punch. "We have both lost our jobs and that means we won't have as much money. We need to save, many things won't be as easy as before."

"How come you don't have jobs?" asked Martin.

"That's not so easy to explain," my father said. He always looked in his plate when he had something unpleasant to say. He stirred his soup, and it seemed as if he were afraid to look us straight in the eye.

My mother spoke of political convictions that must be changed, because the political situation had changed. We became communist many years ago out of necessity. This was no longer the case.

"Before the war, the communists were the only ones who fought against the Nazis. We were certain then that they were our friends. Today we know we made a mistake. But it's better to acknowledge the mistake now than to continue working with these people against our convictions," my mother said, and it sounded like a speech at a party meeting.

Little Georg started to sway back and forth in his chair and said he didn't want to eat the soup. My mother didn't respond to him and continued to talk of the great changes in the world that would also change our lives. I thought the time had come to interlace my worries with world politics.

"Does that mean you can't get theater tickets anymore?" I asked my father.

He put down his spoon and, for the first time that day, looked directly at me. "Are these your problems, when our whole means of existence has been destroyed?"

He was right, they were my problems, only mine. I had to come up with two tickets by next Tuesday.

Georg was bored and tapped his spoon on the table. I nudged him on his side with my elbow. I didn't want him to draw their attention away. But every activity of my mother's was focused almost entirely on this little one.

"Georg! Behave yourself!" chided my mother. This was the sentence she always used if anything was bothering her. And she said it to anyone, even to my father. If I were upset because she didn't let me go out on Saturday night, or if I put both sausage and cheese on a hard, dried, crispy bread, something she couldn't stand, she almost always used the same sentence. "Peter, behave yourself!"

She came from an upper class family, unlike my father, and grew up in Prague high society. Her father was a chemist, but failed in several attempts to build his own company, and later worked as the director of the Gutmann Bank in Prague. In the few photographs that she saved from the war, one could see large families, with nannies who carried little girls in their arms, noble men in dark suits and women in long dresses.

When my mother was sixteen, her mother arranged for her to escape from Prague before the Germans marched in. My mother fled with a fake birth certificate to England and lived with a Quaker family in Cornwall. There she waited desperately for her mother, who had stayed too long in Prague and could not escape after the Germans occupied the country.

It was a tragic story that always brought tears to my mother's eyes when, even years later, I asked about her mother. Her mother looked after two small children in

Prague whose parents were already abroad searching for the right house in order to begin a new life somewhere. At that time nobody took the situation as seriously as today we know it was. By the time the children's parents had saved their assets abroad and found the right house, the Germans were already in Prague, their children could not get out, and their parents could not return. My grandmother accompanied the children all the way to Auschwitz.

My parents met in Cornwall. My father had fled from Vienna, he had left his parents, too. His mother and his little sister didn't survive the war. His older brother was able to get away to England, and his sister escaped with her music band to North Africa. She now lives in France. The father of my father died shortly after the German invasion.

I tried to find his grave once at the large Jewish cemetery in Vienna, but it was hopeless. I did find a grave under a tangle of bushes and weeds, but the words were no longer legible.

My mother spent the war in London; my father enlisted in the British Army and spent two years in India, where the British had sent him. He often talked about how angry he was at that time, because he wanted to fight at the front in Europe against the Germans. Both came back to Vienna at the behest of the Communist Party after the war in order, as they explained during this memorable meal, to build a new Austria.

"Are you now going to leave the Communist Party?" I asked my parents, while my little brother slowly slid off the bench and crawled under the table. They both nodded, and it looked like they were ashamed. I didn't know whether it was because they had stayed in the party for so long, or because they were leaving now.

We sat in silence, no one was eating anything when the phone rang. My father picked up the phone in the hall, and there was a heavy discussion I only partially understood. My mother was silent and tried to listen. Martin and I were very quiet.

When my father came back, his face was serious, eyes staring, searching in the distance for something to discover.

"That was Herbert," he said to my mother.

"What did he want? To reproach you for your decision?"

My father nodded. Herbert was not the only one who called that Sunday. One after another, friends and colleagues of my parents accused them of treason because they were leaving the party during such a problematic time.

In the afternoon a friend of my mother's dropped by. His name was Lajos, and he had previously been a member of the worker's committee in the same lamp factory where my mother had supervised the cafeteria. He was a small, wiry man, always wearing a Pullman cap on his head, and for my brothers and me he was a replacement for our missing grandfathers. He played soccer with us and told us about his life, which was always full of good material for exciting stories. He had no children, but did have a German shepherd my mother couldn't stand that always lay on the floor in the front room as long as Uncle Lajos was with us.

This time Uncle Lajos didn't want to play with us. He sat with my mother in the living room.

"So, what will you do?" he asked her.

"We quit, none of this business has anything to do with why we joined up back then, so we can't do it anymore."

I was still sitting at the dining table, leafing through a magazine and able to observe the two.

I saw how Lajos began to tremble, his face turning pale. "And Spain, where I lost my best friends? And later Buchenwald, where the rest of them were massacred? And our comrades in the Red Army that liberated us? That was all nothing, that's all just forgotten."

"What does that have to do with the fact that they have occupied my Prague? Just because people want a little more freedom?" replied my mother.

Uncle Lajos stood up. He took a deep breath, tried to say something important, but nothing came out. At that moment my father returned. He had driven our new car to the nearest bakery. He did it almost every Sunday to pick up a few pastries. A week ago, the new car my parents had ordered was delivered to us. It was a Saab, a beautiful dark green car, and they would have been very proud of this beautiful car if they had not lost their jobs.

When Uncle Lajos saw the car my father was parking from the living room window, he found his voice again. "Oh, so that's how it is!" he shouted. "You've already been bought by our enemies. A fine new car and a great salary! You have betrayed your comrades! Oh hell!"

The door opened and my father walked in. He carried a cake wrapped in white paper flat on one hand. "What's wrong, why are you yelling?" he asked Uncle Lajos.

"How can you suddenly afford such a car? Are you working for the right-wing *Kronen Zeitung* now? Have they offered you enough money? Will they pay you a large salary when you curse your former comrades?"

My father was never very good when it came to a dispute. He was, rather, the one who tried to sort things out before they got tangled up in disturbing emotions. But this time the dear uncle seemed to have gone too far. "I think it's better that you go now," he said quietly, the cake still in one hand.

"You'll see!" Uncle Lajos took a step towards my father, who stepped back and now had to hold the cake with both hands.

"Get out!" my mother said quietly, and Uncle Lajos walked without saying a word into the hallway, took his dog and left.

I was still sitting at the dinner table. My father put the cake on the table and once again looked me in the eye. It was the second time today. Then he went into the kitchen and began to fill the coffee pot with water – it was one of those Italian coffee pots, water below, ground coffee in the middle – screwed it tight and put it on the stove. I watched him from the dining room and saw that he screwed on the top without putting any coffee inside.

"You forgot the coffee," I said to him, but so softly he didn't hear me.

He put the pot on the stove, lit the flame and waited in front of the pot until the hot water surged through the nozzle into the upper chamber. Then he lifted the lid and saw that it was only hot water.

In the evening, more friends and acquaintances visited my parents. They all sat together in front of the TV and waited excitedly for the news from Prague. Some had tears in their eyes. I was allowed to stay as the eldest son and sat on a leather seat in a corner at the back of the room.

I couldn't understand why everyone was so shaken up. What had happened? It was like a football game where you stop cheering for the white team and begin to root for the black team.

Ultimately, everything was happening far away from Vienna, the Russians had not come here, and our lives, even with less money, didn't necessarily have to change. In any case, I decided to stop defending the Russians to my friends and classmates and to stop condemning the Americans automatically. This meant that a lot of things would become easier for me.

Around eight o'clock in the evening a special message from Prague was broadcast on TV. We saw tanks rolling through the streets, angry people throwing stones and bottles at the tanks, weeping women and young people trying to climb onto a truck that carried foreign soldiers.

Then my mother sent me to my room. "Go to sleep," she said, smiled and ran her fingers through my hair, which she rarely did.

At the time, I slept and studied in a tiny room on the first floor of our house right next to the staircase. The room was as long as my bed and not more than twice as wide, so there was still space for a small writing table.

I lay awake for a long time and remembered the last May Day celebration when I marched with my brothers and my parents on the Ringstrasse in Vienna. A grandstand was built in front of the Parliament where a few party officials stood in gray suits with red carnations in their buttonholes. They waved to us as we marched past, and someone spoke into a microphone. When we had passed the grandstand, the people around me began to shout a name, like they were calling someone. "Dubček!" echoed across the square, and from a different direction, I heard them shout another name, but I couldn't understand it.

I knew that night, lying in my bed that it was this Dubček the Russians and their allies had overthrown in Prague. And that my parents, who were ruined now, had placed all their hopes in this Dubček.

The next morning my father was already up when I came down the stairs. He had already had breakfast and was in good spirits. He wanted to apply as a spokesman for a photography company, he said as he gathered his briefcase. "Then you can get a camera for free," he told me.

"I don't need a camera, I need theater tickets for the French play," I replied. It just slipped out that way. For some reason I had remembered that on Tuesday evening, tomorrow, I would see Katya again.

For a moment he stood there with a portfolio in his hand that he wanted to put into his briefcase, looked vacantly at a point where there was nothing and nothing would ever be. He slid the portfolio into the briefcase without answering and went into the hallway. I heard him get dressed and then leave the house.

That day at school I was indifferent to the political situation in the world. The large logical system, the division of people into decent and indecent, which guaranteed me a certain political stability over the years, no longer existed and a new one was not in view.

When the history teacher made a remark about the events in Prague, and my classmates turned to me in anticipation that I would as usual give a political explanation of the other side, I disappointed them. I leaned back, grinned and said nothing. What did I care about any of that stuff?

We – that meant the whole family – had quit the party. There was no ideology any more, no sticking together for an idea and no need to defend the comrades. There was not even a future to fight for.

During the break, Otto waddled over to me, a fat, unlikable guy who came to school in a sweaty dark blue tracksuit all year, and whose mother had once asked our teacher to seat her son far away from me, since my communist ideas might be dangerous for him. He had been sitting two rows behind me for a few weeks.

He stood in front of me in his baggy pants. "And? Aren't you fucking communists anymore? Just Jews now?" he asked.

I don't know how it happened or what it was that made me react that way. Until then I had never had any experience with anti-Semitism, had never been insulted or ridiculed. We were not religious Jews, never went to a synagogue. The only reference to our belonging to the Jewish community was the murder of my parents' families. But this morning I got up slowly, glanced at the eyes of my classmate Otto and slapped him on the face with my hand so hard the sound of it reverberated in the classroom. Since he had not expected this, his round, unprotected face hung in front of me like a punching bag.

Otto staggered back; it was suddenly quiet in the classroom, and for a moment I thought everyone else would jump on me. But the bell rang, the next hour began, and everyone returned to their seats.

Otto didn't say another word to me that day, and neither did the others.

The next day – it was Tuesday – I knew when I got up in the morning I had failed. I had not managed to get the theater tickets. Constantly talking to myself, I tried to rehearse a conversation with Katya. I made up my mind to tell her that it was a higher power that had prevented us from going to the theater together.

As it turned into Tuesday afternoon, thoughts about the evening began to torment me. My father was at home, sitting in the living room reading a newspaper. It hadn't gone so well with the interview, he said. At first it had, the head of the PR department who interviewed him had been very impressed by my father's experience. But when he asked where he had last worked, and my father told him at a communist newspaper, that he had resigned because of his convictions, the PR-department head began hesitating and became noticeably cautious. He sent my father home with the usual empty phrase, someone would inform him of the company's decision.

I listened to him for a while and then put on my shoes to go to the Youth Club at the local party headquarters, without theater tickets.

"Where are you going?" asked my mother, who was in the kitchen slicing bread for dinner.

"To the club, it's Tuesday," I replied.

"You're not going to this club anymore, when your parents have broken off all contact with the party –"

"Why not, we only want to play table tennis, same as every Tuesday." I didn't understand what she was trying to tell me.

My father stood up and yelled: "You can't betray us now!"

I was a stubborn sixteen-year-old and would have never accepted such an argument, if not, yes if not for the fact that Katya was waiting for me, and I would have to meet her in a few minutes without the promised tickets. To me, my parents' argument suddenly felt quite logical, after all, they weren't communists any more so why should I remain one? So, I didn't go to the party headquarters.

When I got on the tram the next day to go to school, Katya was standing on the rear platform. This happened at most two or three times a year. She went to another school that was farther away, and we only saw each other when I took a later tram.

She walked towards me, and her face didn't have that gentle, soft expression I loved so much.

"Where were you yesterday?"

"I'm not coming on Tuesday anymore –"

"And? Why not?"

I didn't know what to say. "I don't know. I've been playing table tennis for years, and I'm simply not getting any better."

"Don't be so stupid, I know exactly why you didn't come!"

I stood there with my school bag between my legs. "And?"

She came very close to my face. Kiss her now, I thought to myself, then everything will be fine again. Quick as a flash I pressed my lips to hers and held her head with my right hand to keep her from backing away.

She was so surprised that she didn't move for a few seconds. Then she pressed her body against me, and I felt her tongue try to open my mouth. She pushed it wildly around between my teeth and sucked tight on my lips. This was my first French kiss, and I barely moved so I wouldn't do anything wrong. We both leaned against the wall, and I knew in that moment that I had won her even without the theater tickets.

But suddenly she jerked her head back and pushed me away from her with both hands. We both almost fell. "Are you crazy?"

I didn't understand her behavior and tried to continue to build on the momentum of my good idea.

"You'll see, I'll get the tickets for the French play –"

"You can shove them up your ass, I don't go out with traitors!"

"Traitors? What do you mean?"

"You know. Your parents! My father said we should never have trusted people like you!"

"People like us?"

The tram stopped. The doors opened. Katya's expression hardened, she took her school bag and got out. It wasn't even the right station. ■

PETER SICHROVSKY is an Austrian journalist, author, and former politician. In 1989 he co-founded Austria's liberal newspaper *Der Standard* and was a member of the European Parliament from 1996 to 2004. He is the author of several inter-nationally best-selling books based on interviews, which include *Strangers in Their Own Land: Young Jews in Germany and Austria Today* (Basic Books, 1986) about German and Austrian children of Holocaust survivors and *Born Guilty: Children of Nazi Families* (Basic Books, 1988), which was adapted into theatrical works in over fifteen lang-uages. Other acclaimed works include *Abraham's Children: Israel's Young Generation* (Pantheon, 1991) and a book of interviews with 21st-century German neo-Nazis entitled *Incurably German* (Swan Books, 2001). Sichrovsky was a foreign correspondent between 1986 and 1996 for publications including *Stern Magazine*, the *Sueddeutsche Zeitung*, and *Profil*. Currently he writes for the online magazine *Schlaglichter,* where he is a widely-read columnist. Sichrovsky has published eighteen books in German. This is his first work of fiction that has been translated into English.

SELECT WORKS BY PETER SICHROVSKY

Austsrahlungskraft, Frankfurt: WEKA Verlag, 1981

Krankheit auf Rezept, Cologne: Kiepenheuer u Witsch, 1984

Strangers in Their Own Land (English translation by Jean Steinberg) New York: Basic Books, 1986. Original title: *Wir wissen nicht was morgen wird, wie wissen wohl was gestern war*, Cologne: Kiepenheuer u Witsch, 1985. Translated into five languages, produced as a play in several countries.

Born Guilty (English translation by Jean Steinberg) New York: Basic Books, 1988. Original title: *Schuldig Geboren*, Cologne: Kiepenheuer u Witsch, 1987. Translated into more than ten languages, most recently Chinese (2017), produced as a play and re-written by Ari Roth (Director of Jewish Theatre in Washington), produced as a play in Israel, UK, Australia, Germany, Austria, The Netherlands, France and many other countries.

Seelentraining, Hamburg: Rowohlt Verlag, 1988

Abraham's Children (English translation by Jean Steinberg), New York: Pantheon, 1991. Original title: *Die Kinder Abrahams*, Cologne: Kiepenheuer u Witsch, 1990.

Mein Freund David, Zürich: Nagel u Kimche, 1990, produced as a movie by German TV.

Incurably German (English translation by Angi Janitschek), New York: Swan Books, 2001. Original title: *Unheilbar Deutsch*, Cologne: Kiepenheuer u Witsch, 1993. Produced as a play in Germany.

Die Kobrafalle, Zürich: Nagel u Kimche, 1994

Das Bild vom Roten Drachen, Zürich: Nagel u Kimche, 1995

Der Antifa-Komplex, München: Universitas Verlag, 1998

Kafka's Fall, Wien: Ibera Verlag, 2001